OF MATE[illegible]IC

a magical small tow[illegible] romance

MAGGIE FRANCIS

a magical small town romance

# of MATES & MAGIC

Eliza Falls book one

Maggie Francis

Of Mates & Magic

a magical small-town romance
Eliza Falls book one

Maggie Francis

COVER DESIGN: JM Design
DEVELOPMENTAL EDITOR: Brenna Davies Editing
COPY EDITOR: Amy Ollerton

Maggie
FRANCiS
magical small town romance

www.maggiefrancis.com

For G
Despite it all.

For A&H
Always and forever, no matter what.

Chapter 1

Cora

The pile of invoices stacked on top of the box in my hands slides ominously close to the edge as my fingers clench on the sides, a skittering of awareness dancing up my spine. I stumble, my shoulders twitching as I inhale sharply, the top few pages making a break for freedom. I jerk my body to the side, attempting to correct the trajectory of the paperwork, cringing at the sound of the bottles clinking inside the box. Narrowly avoiding disaster, I manage to contort my body into the correct angles to catch the rogue papers and set the package on the counter in front of me. I take a deep, slow breath in through my nose to settle myself and take my hands off the box.

"He's staring at you again."

"What?" I look up sharply at the sound of Desi's voice.

We're working behind the counter, getting a couple of packages prepped to ship out. Desi and I have owned and run this boutique together for the last few years. Some people say that you shouldn't go into business with your best friend, but Desi and I balance each other out perfectly. Desi is a bundle of cheerful, effervescent energy, all sweet smiles and warmth. I lean more towards being a bit (ok, a lot) awkwardly antisocial and generally cagey. I excel behind the scenes, handcrafting most of our apothecary inventory and managing the accounts of other artists we carry. While I am happy to work with customers and provide a friendly, if quietly mundane shopping experience, Desi is our customer service witch. Quite literally. She is a spirit witch, her gifts allowing her to see to the heart of a person's desires and provide them with the exact interaction they need. Her magic is more than that too, bordering on some classic fortune teller vibes. It makes her a favourite with locals and tourists both, setting the tone for our place in the community here in Eliza Falls. Her gifts came with a warning though. When her magic gives her a vision, there is no getting around it.

My gifts on the other hand, are a little more… extroverted. I have earth magic. I can control the elements.

Sort of.

I have wind. Not the gassy kind thank you very much! More like a little gust of wind that lives inside of me. That I am *mostly* in charge of. It's warm and pushy and often wants to come out to play when I am not ready to deal with it. And the fire, let's not forget about that fun little number. Oh no, not just the "fire in my belly" kind like some people say in regards to my temper, but, like, actual flames that spark out of my hands. That I can mostly sort of control?

It's a mixed bag of very obvious paranormal activity that I would rather keep to myself. An issue that I have worked hard over the years to stay on top of. So I hold it close. Unless I am working on something that actively needs my magic, I wrap it up tight and lock it up deep inside me.

"He's totally into you; look at him *mooning* at you!" Desi hisses behind me again.

Ugh.

I look up and search out the dark brown eyes I know are looking at me. On the other side of the cobbled courtyard, a space filled with benches, potted plants and flowering trellises, sure enough, he is there.

Sebastian O'Connell.

Good grief he is hot.

Broody, grumbly, hulking with masculine muscles and Hot with a capital H.

He and his brother moved into our little town last year and he's been popping up out of the corner of my eye ever since. He's intense, and a little weird… I smile at him and he visibly blusters and darts his eyes away, his flushed cheeks noticeable from here. Trying to pretend he wasn't just staring at me maybe? Or perhaps I have something in my teeth?

Running my tongue across my teeth and turning around to look at Desi, I also make sure my fly is zipped.

Sartorial mishaps happen people!

But nope. As far as I can tell, my pants are done up and my teeth are clean. Seb just glowers at me from time to time.

"He's always glowering at you! He's so adorable." Desi says.

"Don't read my thoughts, and he's not adorable. He's weird." I reply.

"I'm not reading your thoughts, Cora. You're muttering again." She sings at me, grinning her beautiful grin.

UGH.

Turning around to look at him again, I notice that his brother is with him. Just like Desi and I, the two men are thick as thieves but also night and day. Where Seb is growly and broody and generally quiet, his brother Tate is a bundle of dude-bro energy and a ray of fucking sunshine.

It was annoying.

But considering that Tate channels that positivity toward running the volunteer program at the local animal rescue and rehab center and fosters some of the more intense rescues, I couldn't really bitch about it. He uses his talents and energy to support our little town and complaining about that says more about me than anything else.

It's not his fault that I am an antisocial weirdo, and that talking to hot guys sends me skittering into my awkward place.

We all have one. Or at least most of us do I'm sure. It can't just be me that gets tongue-tied, red-faced and squeaky whenever a cute specimen of the opposite sex makes eye contact.

Right?!

Desi chuckles quietly behind me again while I let my stormy thoughts get the best of me and I turn back around to look across the courtyard again. Tate is waving happily at us and Desi sunnily waves back.

"Oh, I have got to get myself over there and snuggle that man! Gah! His whiskers kill me."

I scowl a little bit at the men some more, watching Seb try to wrangle his ridiculously smiley brother out of the patio that they are sitting at. Tate throws his head back laughing and Seb's shoulders are high around his ears. I can practically hear him grumbling. I frown, realizing that now I am the one staring and give myself a little shake. I'd like to know more about him. I'd like to be cool and say something smooth and impressive, but my awkwardness and Seb's general gruff grumpiness have prevented the two of us from actually talking to each other. There is something about him that tugs at me, but I can't quite put my finger on it.

My hair tickles across my eyes and I absently push my hand into it to get it out of my face. It dances across my nose again and I stiffen. My stupid wind is flaring and I inhale sharply, clapping my hands over my head and swinging my glare around to Desi.

"I know Cupcake, go try that new lavender and chamomile roll-on that came in the other day, I tucked one onto your workbench for you." Her smile is serene, not in the least bit affected by my magically stressed hair.

I dash to the back and pull the elastic from my braid as I go, my pink locks floating around my shoulders. I take deep breaths and count to five for each inhale and exhale. A trick that my mom taught me back in kindergarten. I close the door to my workroom behind me and sink into the velvet rolling chair that I saved up for, the plush emerald green filling me up with satisfaction. Another one of my tricks is to focus on the little things that bring me joy, and that fancy chair was the first purchase I made for myself once the shop was making money. Every time I sit in it, I feel like a legit boss babe and I love every indulgent stitch of it.

It only takes me another few minutes to get my magic under control and I pull my long hair into a tight topknot, secure it with the elastic and roll my shoulders.

I've got this.

Most humans don't really know that magic exists.

It's the job of every supernatural being to keep it that

way, but considering the population of our small town, there are a disproportionate amount of us magical folks to humans. Most of our locals are in on it. Eliza Falls runs a brisk tourist trade in a cheekily magical way. It's not ever broadcast as real magic, but we let the tourists think what they will. Our shop, Brick & Mortar, carries a combination of real and imagined occult items; teas and tinctures, tumbled semi-precious stones and a gorgeous selection of talismans and amulets for all of your real or imagined magical needs. Supernatural locals toe a fine line between encouraging the economy and protecting our community. No one really wants to get the wrong kind of attention.

I've seen the *X Men*. I've seen *Splash*.

Some humans can be trouble with a capital T.

Shaking my head, I walk back out to the front desk and look over at my best friend. She's leaning against the top of the front display with her chin in her hand, openly watching the O'Connells as they start to get themselves to their feet.

"Girl, you guys aren't dating. Hopping over there for a snuggle would be questionable."

"Yeah but just look at him." She sighs, straight-up fangirl mooning at him from inside our shop.

"He can see you, he was just waving at you." I snark.

"I know! Isn't he dreamy! What sharp eyes he has. I wonder how his teeth will feel nibbling me all over." Desi sighs dramatically again and flounces into the back room to get another shipping label for the printer.

Across the courtyard, Seb rolls his eyes at his brother and grumbles something at him as they get up to leave. He throws another look at me over his massive shoulder, the eye contact sending a thrill up my spine (gah!) before he and his brother clear their table and walk out.

My ears feel hot and I can tell my cheeks are likely

flushed as pink as my hair. I try to shake the feeling off, literally giving my body another little shimmy. Then I cough a little puff of smoke and turn tail to run to the back room for a glass of water. Seb's eyes are stirring up some feelings and I'm not sure how to react.

Chapter 2

Seb

"Dude, just go talk to her." Tate cheerfully taunts me. My brother thinks everything is easy. He is open and friendly and I… it's not that easy for me.

Especially with her.

I felt her almost immediately when we moved into this funny little town. Coming to Eliza Falls wasn't always the end destination, we'd been travelling together and letting the wind tell us where to go for the last couple of years. Following a feeling that nipped and tugged at me, pulling me towards something that I couldn't see. Tate was generally happy to follow where I led. We have always been like that, ever since we were scrappy cubs terrorizing our long-suffering grandparents. Well, terrorizing might be a strong word… we were just kids doing the things that kids do, but Gramps and Gamma were old and quiet and they raised us after our parents left.

The old ache in my chest pulsed as I thought about

them, my head thumping in time with my heart and my Wolf growling at the pressure.

Tate didn't know it, but all our years of wandering weren't just random exploration. I was hoping to find a trace of *something* that would lead me to our parents. I snarled as the familiar headache spread down to my shoulders. Any time I tried to follow the thought of them or where they might be, a sense of wrongness swept over me and the thoughts would vanish. We've covered a lot of the North American continent, but after wandering for so long, Gamma had suggested that we spend some time with our aunt.

Aunt Jett has a farm here in this kooky little town. She's lived here as long as I can remember; memories of her smiling, wrinkled face go all the way back as far as my unreliable memory goes. I don't know why the memories of Jett are so clear but the thoughts of my mom slip away from me like smoke under a door, but it sets my teeth on edge and I have to shake my head to clear it.

Aunt Jett calls her home a farm. I would call it a big backyard with some chickens in it. They are terrifying in their attitude, strutting around like they own the place, more often than not creating a mess inside the house. But Aunt Jett has given them flowery and illustrious names like The Duke and The Empress so I guess they are pet chickens? Can you have a pet chicken?

Aunt Jett loves them so they are a part of the scene here. I think Tate likes them, but I just want to eat them.

"Seriously dude. She's noticed you too. We can talk to them together. I want to snack on Desi." Tate waggles his eyebrows at me.

"Leave her friend alone."

"I don't know man, there's a pull there. That Desi is delicious. She makes my ears tingle."

I snort at my brother and keep walking back to Aunt Jett's. The house is at the far end of town. An old, rambling, tumble of a house with a wrap-around porch and string lights in rainbow colours all over the yard. I don't know how she managed to get the lights through all the apple trees, but they flicker and twinkle all year round across the whole property. I don't even know where she has them plugged in.

Aunt Jett is a character. She's been in that old house her whole life, it was her parents before she married Uncle Frank. And they happily hunkered down in it when her folks decided that they were ready to settle down into a little cabin by the beach.

Uncle Frank had passed ten years ago now and Aunt Jett is settling into her Little Old Ladyhood with a ferocious determination. She makes apple butter from the trees in the yard, knits hideous and itchy scarves for anyone she can get her hands on and collects cookbooks like they're stamps.

Tate seems happy here in this funny little town. He makes connections easily and people lean towards him like he keeps magnets in his pockets.

I… don't so much. I'm not as easy to talk to.

Or at least, my Wolf isn't...

Tate and I are weres. We both shift into wolves. Not like a creepy Halloween werewolf. Like actual wolves. It's not as gory as the movies make it look. It's more like a shimmer of magic and less like a crunch of bone and tearing muscle. It's like water flowing over river rocks. My Wolf flows out of me and we trade shapes. I'm still there when my form is a Wolf. Just like my Wolf is always there when I stand as a man. We are the same. Ish.

My Wolf doesn't talk to me in words, but in instincts.

Like when we met *her*.

....

Tate and I had only just moved into Jett's carriage house attached to the old garage the week before. The three of us were standing in her kitchen, Jett stirring something on the stove that smelled suspiciously like caramel and Tate was eating an apple that he had picked from the gala tree in the backyard. He and I hadn't been off the property since we arrived, I was edgy and tired, frustrated to have lost the trail of what I was looking for again. Jett had been feeding us since we arrived and Tate and I had started repairing some of the old built-in cabinets in the front room as a thank you for letting us stay here with her.

I sat quietly at the island behind her nursing a glass of cold water and Tate leaned against the counter on her left, chatting happily around mouthfuls of apple. Aunt Jett slapped his hand away every time he tried to dip a finger into the sauce.

"Knock it off, you little stinker!" She snapped, bumping him away a third time with her apron-clad hip. She went back to stirring her sauce and Tate grinned at her.

"I need you boys to go down to Butter My Muffin."

Tate choked on the bite of the apple he had and my mouthful of water sprayed all over the island in front of me and down my chin.

Coughing and dripping, I got up to pound on my brother's back, his face red and sputtering. But Jett swung around with a wooden cutting board and whacked the apple out of his mouth.

"WHAT?!" he croaked out.

"Butter My Muffin." she repeats, eying her cutting

board before putting it back on the counter. She turned and held my gaze unblinking, like I was the one suddenly talking nonsense.

I knew that Jett had gotten a little odd in her solitude here in the last few years. But surely not so lonely that she would… proposition us for oral sex. She's not actually our biological aunt, she's Gamma's best friend from childhood and has been everyone's aunt over the years. But this is way out of the scope of her usual weirdness. The water I had spit out all over myself was dripping off my chin, the drops hitting the floor as loud as thunder in the awkward silence.

"Walter usually delivers the goods but I'm feeling like I don't want to wait for it today." She continues. I started to think that I was having an out of body experience. Jett keeps saying words, but their meaning refuses to make sense.

"Walter, um, butters your muffin?" Tate coughed out. The drink in my hand sloshed as I twitched in my confusion.

"Aunt Jett." I started slowly. "What *exactly* are you asking us to do?"

She looked between us as if we were stupid, like explaining her sexual proclivities to us was not something out of the ordinary.

"Walter, Sela and I have an arrangement."

Oh Gods, this was more than I needed to know this early in the morning. But there's a piece missing in all of this that I couldn't quite put my finger on, so I pressed on.

"What, exactly, is the arrangement?"

Jett tilted her head and huffed impatiently.

"My girls lay the best eggs in all of Eliza Falls. So in exchange for a couple dozen every week, I get a standing order of hot cross buns delivered. Every Saturday afternoon. But I've got a hankering to enjoy a fresh bun with a cuppa right now, so take your big forearms into town and pick them up for me. This doesn't seem very confusing to me."

I blinked at my brother and watched his eyes register with understanding.

"Aunt Jett, what is the name of Walter's bakery?"

"Butter My Muffin. I was very clear. Do you boys need a few more days to settle in? You both look a little peaky around the edges."

One of the fluffiest chickens I had ever seen wandered into the kitchen then and Jett bent over to scoop it up, pressing it against her chest and muttering about us being obtuse as she shuffled out of the room.

We stared at each other for a beat before Tate burst out laughing. I shook my head and pulled my wet shirt off as I stepped out the door to the back porch. The carriage house that we were staying in was in that corner of the yard and I went in for a dry shirt. Tate was waiting for me in the driveway when I came back out.

"I think the bakery is closed right now while they work their booth at the market, let's swing by there first." Tate said.

We wandered out and headed towards the open-air market that the main square in town held every weekend. We'd seen the signs when we were dropping the empty moving boxes off at the hardware store. Old Jim, the owner, had a couple of crafty grandkids and Aunt Jett made sure we knew to drop the boxes off when we were done.

We were nearly at the market when my Wolf pricked his ears. I could smell her before I saw her. It's not as creepy as it sounds I swear. It was like… coming home. All of my senses calmed and jumped to high alert at the same time. I felt dizzy and I looked sharply over at Tate, who was looking at me with a shocked expression on his face.

"Dude, you're bristling. What gives?"

I shook my head to clear it and that's when I saw *her*.

She was under a market tent with a bubbly redhead. They had their heads bent together over something in front of them, quietly arguing. She shook her hair off her shoulder and the scent of her washed over me like a tidal wave.

I grunted and locked my legs in place, like a wrestler getting ready for their next opponent. My Wolf was preening though, he hummed inside me and was pushing to get closer to her. He knew, without a doubt, who she was.

Ours.

Weres have a Mate Bond that connects them to their perfect Mate. It sounds like a cheesy fairy tale the way that some old wolves talk about it, but I had never really thought about it much. Tate was a romantic and liked to speculate about the idea every now and again, but I had always brushed it off as nonsense.

I was standing corrected now. My Wolf was practically prowling inside my skin, aching to get closer to her.

But we had just moved to this town and we had no idea who she was.

I looked at her, I was probably staring. I could hear Tate saying words but I wasn't listening to what those words were. All of my attention was focused on her.

She was tall and trim and had pink hair. It was wavy and a little frizzy and as I watched her she threw it up into a messy bun on the top of her head. She and the redhead were working together to fix something on the table they had set up in their market stall. They were selling something at the market. Maybe she was a farmer?

I had taken a few halting steps towards her without realizing it and she caught the movement out of the corner of her eye. She looked up at me and I froze. Her eyes were big and dark and she wore a deep blue eyeliner that made her look smokey and a little dangerous.

But then her nose scrunched up, like she was concentrating on something, and her little white teeth appeared. Less dangerous.

"Can I help you?' She asked me suddenly.

"Uh…" I muttered. Still staring idiotically at her.

She pulled her chin back while she watched me, her eyebrows drawing down like she was waiting for me to not be awkward. But I didn't stop. My eyebrows furrowed and I grunted something.

I GRUNTED AT HER, what was I doing??

She scowled at me then and arched an eyebrow as she turned away. Tate had watched this whole exchange and clapped me on the shoulder.

"Smooth bro. That was very cool."

He walked closer to the two women and leaned against their table.

"Did the WIFI crap out on your chip reader?" He asked them.

My M… *She* looked at him from under smooth eyebrows and looked to her friend. The redhead beamed at Tate and shook her curly hair behind her shoulder.

"We forgot to charge it, and we need to get an extension cord so we can process sales before the market opens." she replied, smiling the whole time.

I couldn't stop staring at her, and she could tell. She kept glancing at me and frowning.

I was fucking this up. Badly. We needed to go. My Wolf snarled at that, he didn't want to leave her now that we'd found her.

"Ugnh." I cleared my throat, I tried again

"Hi."

She watched me struggle, pursed her plump lips to one side.

"Are you ok? " She quietly asked me, her expression made it clear that she was pretty sure I wasn't.

"We need buns." I blurted out in response.

Her eyes widened and I heard Tate snort behind her.

"Ok, that's our cue," He said, nodding his head at the red-haired woman and leaning towards her briefly. Then he swung his arm over my shoulder and pulled me away from the booth. I still hadn't pulled my eyes away from her and my Wolf was scrabbling and whining inside my chest. Desperate to stay near our Mate now that we'd found her.

Her lip was curled up on one side now, a look of confusion on her face as she watched Tate pull me away. I stumbled and finally turned around so I wouldn't trip and make her first impression of me even worse.

"That went well!" Tate said.

....

The last year has been agony. Every time I try to get closer to Cora, I manage to fuck it up. Over and over again I have made the decision that this is it, today is the day that I will actually speak to her, and not just loom at her from a distance like a stalker. But every time I get close, her scent floats over me, calming all the extra sensory stimulation that usually drives me to distraction and I freeze. Feeling that calm wash over me is so rare, so luxurious, that I just want to bask in it. In her. So I clam up, my muscles get tight, my voice deserts me and I end up only making things between us worse. She's so lovely. She doesn't want a broken Wolf like me. She doesn't even know that I am a werewolf.

Werewolves in general are pretty rare, there aren't a lot of us anymore. We tend to keep ourselves under the radar as much as we can. My family pack was small, growing up I only remember my grandparents and Tate. I don't remember much of my parents, other than that Mom was our alpha. Until she wasn't. My memories around them are foggy, slippery and dark. I remember their scents mostly, but after all these years without them, even that small thing is leaving me.

I shake off my melancholy and look back over my shoulder once more while I push my brother out of the patio area. I can see her through the window of her shop, both women are still watching us. Desi with a smirk and Cora with a frown.

Chapter 3

Cora

I hike my bag a little higher on my shoulder and balance the tray of fancy lattes as I walk back to the shop. Desi and I have lived together in the apartment above it for the last couple of years, finding that being so close to everything in town just makes our days so much smoother. To balance out all that together time, I make regular trips to the trails on the far side of town on my lunch breaks and sometimes even first thing in the morning. Desi is not as early a riser as me, so I often get a little window of time on my own most mornings. But there are still some days where only the actual breeze in your face will do. Today was one of those mornings. and I'm heading back to the shop after a perfect autumn walk through gleaming, golden foliage crunching underfoot. The sky is a brilliant cerulean blue, no clouds in sight, and the maples transforming from their lush and verdant green to vibrant ruby and gold fill my soul to the brim with happiness. I smile as I pass Old

Jim sweeping said leaves off of the walk in front of the hardware store, his creased, brown face smiling back at me.

"What incredible thing have the kids built this week Jim?" I ask him as I slow my pace to hear his response. He chuckles and shakes his bald head.

"The little assholes built a catapult out of the treehouse I made for them when they were little. They shot my Josie's rose garden full of chicken shit they stole from Jett's place."

I bark out a surprised laugh and nearly snort.

"Was it Phoebe leading the ring this time?" I ask, picturing seven-year-old Phoebe Jackson and her mischievous little face.

"Sure was, Jace stole the shit in the dark the night before and they defended themselves by saying that it was to fertilize the garden in time for frost. That little stinker is going to make one hell of an engineer one day. My Josie forgave them immediately of course and they were treated to ice cream and fresh cookies."

"That sounds about right." I reply, smiling broadly. "Have a wonderful day Jim."

He nods to me as I pass and I hear him humming to himself all the way from around the corner.

Our shop is located in the center courtyard in town, a sweetly charming, brick-walled, shutter-covered windows and friendly neighbour having, slice of heaven. I take a deep breath in and let my contentment settle into my bones. This is going to be a good day. I can feel it.

"I think we should look at getting some new displays built." Desi says the moment I walk into the shop. I look around at our baby. This little shop is our big dream. Ever since we were teenagers and had watched *Practical Magic,* we both knew we wanted to own a magical apothecary like Sandra Bullock's character. All that light and greenery in the windows. Helping people with quiet magic. It made our souls sing.

Our shop was our own, obviously. Not the same as a fictional character's. But that scene is definitely our inspiration. We carry local skincare products and cater to the town's booming tourist trade with prepackaged bundles with names like "Lovers Lotion" and "Soul Spice". We support our artisan community by building a shopping experience that showcases the talent of our locals.

Desi runs the front of the shop. My own contribution is quieter. Like me. I don't excel at customer service like Desi does. I can hold my own when I'm in the shop by myself obviously, I'm not a monster. But where Desi enjoys and blossoms in the face of groups of people, I prefer the stillness of our workroom.

I make herbal tea blends and potions.

Yes, I know, how apropos. An earth witch making potions. It's not like I cackle over a cauldron in the middle of the woods. I mean, sometimes I chuckle when I am listening to a funny podcast while I stir something in a pot. But it's not the same. I swear.

My magic is simmering herbs in purified oils and infusing chocolate with intention. A lot of what I make for our shop doesn't look any different from some of the beautiful products you can find at human boutiques. But since I have the ability to add a little bit of extra actual magic into my products, I am able to help people a little more.

"What are you thinking of re-merchandising?" I ask, turning to look at her.

"I think we need to do something different with that side display. Your salves are selling well, but I think we can display them better and add a section for your new tea line."

I look over at where she is pointing and think about it.

"I can see that. Something in a light wood with clean lines?" I muse out loud.

"Exactly!" She replies, clapping her hands.

"I'll call Tate and get them to come over and measure the space." She says casually as she walks away from me.

"Wait, what?! *Seb* and Tate? I am sure they're too busy. It's a super busy time for them. Like, crazy busy." I wring my hands and start sweating. Gah! Why am I literally sweating over this?

"Honey Girl, they are not too busy. This is their business. Why wouldn't I call them. They are the best carpenters for miles around and dreamboats to boot! I fully support your crush on Seb. We can bring them iced tea when they get too hot and watch them take their shirts off." Desi swoons.

"Oh my Gods, Desi! They will not take their shirts off!" I shriek.

Just then the front door opens and my mother swoops in in all her glory.

"Oooh! Who is taking their shirts off, Darlings?" My mother purrs at us, sweeping past me and kissing my cheek before doing the same to Desi. Desi turns around and hugs my mother and they giggle like children when I scowl at them both. My mother is a powerful artifact witch. She can imbue objects with magic. She makes jewellery that protects the wearer like in a video game. Rings of power or a necklace that makes you prosperous, stuff like that. We carry her work in the shop and our clientele love her. It doesn't hurt that she has a big personality and loves all of the attention.

"Seb and Tate, Alma, those delicious carpenters from across town." Desi tells her.

"Oh, those boys!" My mother exclaims "How wonderful. They are something to look at aren't they, My Chickadees?"

She turns in a swirl of scarves and tinkling bracelets as she shucks off her jacket and strides for the back room.

"I have a good feeling about those two. If I were twenty years younger I would have seduced them both by now." She throws over her shoulder.

"Ohmygods, MOM, you are too much today!" I holler after her.

Desi just laughs and grabs a box of new mugs from behind the counter and starts to check them off against the inventory list she has stacked on top. Grumbling under my breath as I head back to make sure my mother has what she needs so she can get out of here already, I stop abruptly.

Seb *is* an excellent carpenter. Why can't they come and work in my shop for a week or two and build us a beautiful custom piece? We are both adults. I can be around other adults who are working for me and not drool all over them. I can keep my magic on lockdown when they are around. I can be cool. I will be cool.

Tell that to the trickle of sweat running down my spine.

Mom is unpacking little jewellery boxes from her bag as I step into the back room with her, pulling each one out, lining them up along my workbench. The work surface is clean and tidy, all of my herbs and crystals organized in neat little drawers for easy access. I watch her pull open a couple and pull out a black onyx touchstone. She wraps it up in her hand for a moment, and I can feel her magic building, a frisson of awareness that sweeps up my body. I wait, knowing that she is setting her intention into the stone. She blinks her eyes open and releases a deep breath, before nodding once and handing it to me.

"Keep that in your pocket, Love, it will come in handy."

"Come in handy for what, Mom? Onyx is a protection stone, what do I need protection from?"

She squints at me, her narrowed eyes boring deep into my soul.

"Do you remember that time that you and Desi cast those spa spells in my bathroom when you were seven?"

What? Ok, she's going to make me work for it today.

"Yes, Mom, how can I forget? My hair has been pink ever since." I cross my arms over my chest and lean my hip against my work table. That weekend sleepover was the proverbial straw that broke the camel's back for my dad.

.....

Desi and I were always together. Since the first day of kindergarten, when Desi had walked over to me and whispered "Hello dearest friend" into my ear, and I loved her with all my whole five-year-old heart. We were just always together after that. My mother indulged us, taking Desi under her wing and essentially raising her alongside me as if we were sisters.

Desi's parents had died a couple years before, and her grandfather, GG, became like a second grandpa to me too. If we weren't creating chaos together at my house, we were being angels at GG's.

My dad is, was, human. I am not sure if he's even alive, since he left us shortly after the Great Hair Dying explosion of Second Grade. It was innocent enough, Desi and I had found a book of beauty spells that had arrived in the mail for my mom, and we could not get our hands into it fast enough. Dad wasn't home that afternoon, I don't remember where he was, but it was just Desi and I upstairs in their bathroom, while my mom was out back in the garden. She was deep into casting something so we knew that this was our chance to try out the new spellbook.

Desi wanted to try the blush spell, but we didn't have all of the listed ingredients, so we settled on the hair spell. Being seven and impulsive, neither of us read the fine print explaining that this was permanent change magic. And when we chose pink because it was our favourite colour at the time, neither of us considered that we might change our minds on Monday.

We did mine first because I was secretly envious of Desi's beautiful, copper hair and was hoping that she would leave it. Mine was a mousy, medium brown, so I felt excited about trying pink for the weekend.

We made a terrible mess, the spell requiring a lot of liquid ingredients, one of which was highly reactive, culminating in a smallish explosion that may have permanently stained the countertop and part of the ceiling a vibrant raspberry. Our giddy shrieking called my mom in from the garden while we were frantically cleaning it up, and my once boring hair was now a deep and glossy, rosy pink.

Mom had laughed, smiling at us until she read the spell over and then sitting me down to inform me that my hair was now going to grow in this colour. Forever.

That's when my dad came home and our fun afternoon took a turn.

He hadn't known that Mom was a witch when they had hooked up all those years before. But when she discovered that she was pregnant at nineteen, she had tracked him down to let him know that she was planning to keep me. When he told her that he would stand by her and suggested they try to be together for me, Mom told him about magic. I think he did his best, but he was a pretty conservative guy and once I was born and it was clear that my magic was not a quiet one, he started shutting down. Oh, he was always kind, but even as a child, I knew that he was ashamed of me. We rarely visited with his side of the family and I suspected that he didn't want to have to tell them about our "Little Secret." My mother hated that and made a point to embrace her magic a little more and prove something. Once Desi and I had pinked the bathroom and my hair, something that I couldn't hide, he'd had enough.

Desi and I were sent out to the garden, but we could hear them arguing from inside.

That night at bedtime, Dad had hugged me a little tighter than usual, and was gone when I woke up. I haven't seen him since.

.....

I clear my thick throat, looking up towards the upper shelves to contain the salty tears threatening to spill. I don't think about my dad too often anymore, but whenever I do, it reminds me that I am too much. My magic is too chaotic. It reminds me to squash those feelings deep down inside so they can't make anyone else leave. Repress, repress, repress.

"What does the onyx have to do with my unsuccessful hair spell?"

"Oh nothing darling, but it's good to shore up those

barriers. Something is in the air, I can feel it. It's exciting and scary. So, armour up, Darling!"

I roll my eyes and tuck the little black stone into my shirt pocket. Mom has a habit of being obtuse as hell, so I just chalk it up to mom being mom.

Chapter 4

Seb

I'm sanding down the corner of a custom sideboard getting delivered tomorrow. The joins are smooth and everything is finishing up beautifully. Once I finish sanding, I'll rub in some special oil we use to complete each piece.

This will be perfect timing so I can sit it under the window to catch a little moonlight before the client receives it. This isn't a spell or anything. I just believe that it is good energy. The moon is a benevolent mistress most nights, and letting her caress my work before it goes out into the world feels good in my bones.

Tate thinks it's cheesy. But since I'm the one working tonight, he can shove it. Besides, he runs the business end of things for us, while I do most of the actual carpentry. He and I stumbled into this business shortly after we moved here. Jett's carriage house had been neglected since Uncle Frank passed away, the decade of inattention showing in the old building's sagging porch and crumbling drywall. As a thank you for letting us stay with her, Tate and I spent the first few months here in Eliza Falls fixing the place up. We replaced most of the tired kitchen and rebuilt the porch steps. Once we were finished with that, neighbours started asking us to do odd jobs around town and we built O'Connell Woodworks into the thriving business it is today.

It doesn't hurt that our werewolf nature gives us a boost in strength, allowing us to haul a little extra each trip and make each job wrap up a little faster than expected. Or that Tate's good nature and charm make people seek him out. We have a waitlist of clients and projects lined up that will keep us busy for the next year, and the locals are happy to wait until we can get to their projects. We had to rent a space in town to open an official office and workspace since we've had so many larger custom orders, on top of the smaller special pieces that are my personal preference.

Tate splits his time between managing our orders here and running the volunteer program at the animal shelter. He's always had a way with animals, and this arrangement suits him. The man himself saunters into the workspace not long after I finish the last coat of oil on the sideboard and leans against the opposite workbench.

"We've got a new order," he states. He watches me as I toss the cloth I've been using. I'll deal with it tomorrow. Bad habit, I know, but my Wolf started rumbling as soon as Tate walked in, and I need to give him my undivided attention it seems.

"Are you going to tell me what it is, or do I have to guess?"

Tate's face brightens up into a shit-eating grin and he crosses his arms over his chest.

"Desi called tonight and commissioned some custom

displays for their shop. A solid week or two of on-site work."

I stiffen. My whole body is on high alert. My Wolf is pacing inside, fur bristling at the idea of spending some concentrated time with Cora.

"A custom display? What, what are they looking for?" I grit out.

A whole week, possibly two, is going to be torture. I don't think I can be in close quarters with Cora and not turn into a caveman. My Wolf and I have been managing all this time because of sheer will. And distance. Not being near her is easier to manage because I'm able to hightail it out of there if my Wolf got too close to the surface. I am desperate to connect with her, but every time I get around her I fuck it up and she must think I am…intense. At best.

Every time I try to talk to her, I mostly end up awkwardly hovering over her and glowering because my Wolf wants to roll around all over her and mark her as ours. I fight the instinct because she has never indicated that she wants to be rolled on. Oh gods, now I have a hard-on thinking about rolling her under me.

What she would feel like, what she would sound like as I run my hands all over her lithe body.

I cough to cover the rumbling purr coming from my chest, turning around to shift the tools around on the bench behind me and adjust my dick.

Tate knows about my feelings for Cora. He's known from that first day at the market last year. There's no keeping that kind of secret between us. He felt the energy of my Wolf discovering our true Mate just as I did. His Wolf will protect her because she's Pack. Because she's mine. But I want, no, I *need* Cora to choose me for herself and not just be swept up into the pull of my Wolf magic. I've spent too long feeling alone and outcast to allow myself to assume that she will just swoon into my life. Our family Pack is so small that the idea of a Mate feels like a dream. And I have observed enough of Cora to understand that she holds herself apart. I don't think she opens up to everyone. I have to let her come to me. My Wolf understands that I need this and is patient. He knows that we will protect her and that she deserves time. Humans don't know about us and shifting into my Wolf in front of her won't make her swoon into my arms.

I shake my head to clear it and look over my shoulder at Tate.

"I don't think this is a good idea. I don't think I can control my Wolf if I am around her every day."

"You can. I have a feeling about those two. I think they can handle a little extra." He countered.

"What?" I reply sharply. "What do you mean?"

"There is something about them. Whenever I'm around Desi my ears tingle. It's like my own spidey-sense."

My eyes widen as I take that in. Could Cora be more than human? Is she like me? I push my thoughts back to our interactions over the last year and try to remember if I scented anything different about her. To be honest, I can't really tell, I've spent so much time repressing the shit out of my Wolf in an attempt to not freak her out that even the calming effect she has on me, the fact that I can finally breathe easily around her, has suppressed my observations of her true scent. I have been so blindsided by the Mate Bond that I hadn't even considered her nature. I just assumed that she was human and let myself get swept up in the idea of her. I have watched her from a distance for so long that I think that I know her. But how can I really, until I let her know me?

"When do they want us to start?" I ask.

Chapter 5

Cora

I measure out the lavender in careful scoops. This tea blend is a popular one in the shop, and I am restocking our nearly sold-out shelf of it. It's a calming blend, with lavender, chamomile and cardamom. As I pour the measured blossoms into the glass bowl with the rest of the ingredients waiting, I focus my magic into it. Heat travels down my arms and into the hand-carved wooden spoon I hold as I begin to stir the tea ingredients together. My eyes unfocus, and the magic travels from my fingertips and into the dried blossoms.

This will be a good batch.

With my magic humming all around me while I slowly stir everything in the bowl together, I don't hear the footsteps in the front room. I don't hear Desi purring quiet words to whomever has come into our shop. The process of my magic takes a lot of concentration and my focus is almost entirely on what I am doing.

As I slowly come back to myself, feeling the heat of my

magic pull back up my arms and swirl in my belly, I open my eyes, preparing to give a little intention to the small glass jars that will hold the tea, I hear someone clear their throat. A deep, decidedly *masculine* sounding throat.

I gasp and clutch the sides of the big bowl tightly as I whip my head around and look to the front space.

Seb is standing there, watching me. His dark eyes look deep into mine and I feel my cheeks heat with something. Embarrassment? Relief? Want?? Oh Gods, am I still staring back at him? I am. I'm staring at him. Say something. Open your mouth and *say* something!

"Hey, Cora." He says gruffly, saving me from myself. My name slips from his mouth like a caress up my spine, and I shiver. Has he ever said my name before? Has anyone ever said it quite so earnestly??

I clear my throat. Shake myself a little. Clench my fists tight to zip up my magic. Oh shit, did he see my magic?? I get so pulled into it sometimes that I lose time. I don't always know where the edges are when I am working. We needed to get a bell or something on the door. Or a lock on the workroom door, or fucking *close* the damn thing at least!

Blinking as I stare at him, breaking my trance, I clear my throat again.

"Oh, hey." My cool conversation skills are on point.

I press my lips together as I continue to gawk at him. He's wearing frayed jeans that fit his long legs like a second skin, the well-worn denim hugging his thick thighs and riding low on his lean hips. *Stop it, Cora!*

And a button-up navy flannel shirt that makes his dark eyes look greener than usual. Fuck off, he is unreasonably gorgeous. *Seriously, stop it Cora!*

Shaking my head again, I put the big bowl aside and move away from my workstation to stand awkwardly across from him at the front desk. Desi and Tate are chatting easily near the front door.

"Have you guys…"

"We are ready to.."

We start at the same time.

He huffs out a low, rumbling chuckle, running his big hand over the back of his neck and then looks back up at me from under his lashes quickly. I swallow thickly, feeling seduced by that small glance. *Get it together Cora!* I never get sucked into hormones around men like this. Only Seb makes me feel so unhinged. But we've also never been so close together before and I can feel the heat of his big body, smell his laundry soap and evergreen scent like a fog of lust swirling straight to my core.

Good Lords, pull yourself together woman!

"We are here to take some measurements and get an idea of what you'd like the finished piece to look like." He says quickly. He inhales a deep breath and straightens sharply, his nostrils flaring and his body pulling tight. I notice his hands clench at his sides. His brow furrows at the same time as mine does and I lean my body back, just a little.

"Uh, ok great, um. Let's head out front and we can talk about it?" I say, although it sounds more like a question. Why did he shift gears just now?

"Cool." he says gruffly and quickly spins around and heads back out and away from me, shoulders tight. Like he can't get away from me fast enough. What the fuck?

Chapter 6

Seb

I have to get space. This is dangerous.

We are awkwardly talking, the pull I feel towards her making my muscles strain as she looks at me with those big eyes. The effect of being near her is setting my skin on fire and dousing me with cool water at the same time. Her nearness quiets all the noise in my head, all of the sounds my Wolf constantly sorts quieten. I don't need to suppress the stimuli crashing into me. I can focus on just her. She usually smells like lavender and the cotton of her clothing mixed with something a little spicy, her own natural elixir. Soft and warm and welcoming. This time her scent is different, an unexpected undercurrent of something new. I inhale her tantalizing scent, taking a little part of her into myself, and I can feel it in my blood.

She is aroused. By me! As soon as I catch the scent, my whole body pulls tight. My Wolf is pleased. He paces inside me, growling to get out and claim her and I panic. I can feel my muscles bunching under my skin as I spin away from her. I was finally making progress around her, I managed to put several words together into a sentence near her without grunting like an idiot. But I can barely look at her now for all the raging hormones and conflicting desires coursing through me.

She doesn't want this, how could she? She deserves someone who can hold fucking eye contact for more than a second. Someone safe to be around. My Wolf is raging inside me as I force my body into stillness. I can feel my face pull into a frown, my teeth aching with the need to stretch and claim and I hunch my shoulders in on myself. She deserves more than a wild animal snarling at her.

I practically run into the front of the shop, getting as much distance between us as I can to get my Wolf under control. My cock is aching and I have to press my hand hard against it to suppress the raging emotions inside me. She shouldn't see me like this. She would recoil from me if she knew I was reacting to her like this. She deserves more from a Mate than a horny neanderthal with a raging boner. I want her to want *ME*, to need me like I need her, but she doesn't have all the information. She doesn't know that I am a godsdamned werewolf, that my Wolf has decided that she's ours, and that we will never let her go now that we've found her. Chicks love to have wildly unexpected and unbelievable information thrown at them from dudes they barely tolerate.

But she is aroused just now. Or she *was*, before I hulked out and pulled a *Teen Wolf* on her. Maybe…maybe she doesn't just barely tolerate me?

Maybe there is more for her than wariness. Maybe her wariness isn't just because I stare at her like a stalker whenever I see her and can't bring myself to talk to her because I'm afraid to say something preposterous and turn her away from me. I have managed to grunt at her several times and mutter the most random responses to her questions in the past, securing her impression that I am an unintelligible caveman that she should steer clear of.

But maybe…?

I am overthinking. I am also grumbling under my breath and Tate glances up at me as I stalk past him.

His eyebrows lift in a silent question and I snarl back at him in response.

He chuckles at that and follows behind me. We are here to build these women a display for their business. My reactions to Cora are personal and I need to lock that shit up so I can be a fucking professional and get the job done.

I'm just not sure if that is something I, or my Wolf, can do.

Chapter 7

Cora

He ran away from me.

What in all the hells is his deal?! Did I do something or say something that offended him? I look down at myself, I sniff my armpit. I look fine. I don't stink.

What the ever-loving fuck was that?

Through the simmering frustration of my surprise, I realize that my feelings are hurt. I don't like that he just jerked his body ramrod straight and couldn't get away from me fast enough. *He ran away from me*, after we were finally, kind of, talking to each other.

For fuck's sakes. Why do I have to have a crush on the weirdest dude? Because I definitely do. I'm crushing on him hard and I'm not even entirely sure why. I mean, yes, he's intensely good looking, he smells incredible, and his eyes are like dark pools of lost time, and my stupid, selfish vagina wants to get familiar with his big, hard body. But BESIDES ALL OF THAT. We haven't even had a real conversation in the whole time we've known each other. If you could even say that we know each other because anytime we are near each other one of us screws it all up!

Ugh!

But I want to know him. Gods do I want to know him. He is kind, I can tell from the way he talks to *other people* that he is reserved, but his kindness shines through. I've seen him working with Tate's fostered animals, and I am sure he wouldn't like to hear it, but I think it's fucking adorable that he carries orphaned kittens in his shirt pockets. Yes, I have seen him do this. I nearly swooned, TO MY DEATH. And I've seen him around town with kids. He is patient and warm, and those little rug rats flock to him like he is Mother flipping Goose. Only someone with a good heart has that effect on kids like that. Kids know in their bones.

So what is it about me that has him running?

Huffing out a deep breath to try to let my frustration go, I slowly head out to meet him and Tate in the front room. Desi and Tate have no problem yukking it up. I see them as I come into our main space. They're leaning towards each other, the front counter between them, having zero problems with eye contact.

Desi looks my way when I come in, and the look she gives me is one of understanding.

I had briefly mentioned to her that I may have had a tiny crush on Seb months ago and she's been ribbing me about it ever since. But the look on her face today isn't poking fun at me. Something has changed in the last little while, and I wonder just how much she knows. Her gifts aren't as consistent as mine. What I mean is, my magic is like an extension of myself. I can concentrate and my magic will flare or recede in a way that I can control. For the most part anyway. High emotions tend to make it flare and if I've been suppressing it for too long it will find a way out. But if I am careful and pay attention, I am the one in charge of my gift. Desi's magic is more akin to a cat hunting. She'll be minding her own business at the grocery store and suddenly her magic will pounce on her and she'll have a vision. It just depends on what her magic needs her to see. Often she doesn't look like she is in the grip of a magical vision. She'll just tense up a little bit and then shake herself off because the visions are often fast, like a flash of inspiration. And it isn't always a vision like watching a scene in her head. Sometimes it's just a knowing.

Like with us when we were kids. We had met in kindergarten and she just knew that we were important to each other. And we have been, ever since.

She can't predict lottery tickets or anything like that. And she has fully accepted her gifts as a part of her so she never fights it. She is love and light and positivity, her knowing perhaps having given her the sense that her life would be a good one. So she doesn't sweat it. It is sometimes annoying how bright and bubbly she can be, but that is just Desi and I love her.

So, seeing that expression on her face just now makes me feel curious. She knows something and now I just have to let this play out. She won't tell me unless I ask and even then she only tells me what I really need to know, often in riddles because she loves to mess with me. I have a feeling that her gifts are affected by choices, so sometimes things change based on the choices we make. And I can't ask her anything with Tate and Seb right here. Also, I am a grown-up for crying out loud! I can deal with my crush on this weirdo and get on with my day. I can do this. I can! I will walk over there like he isn't bristling at his tool belt lying on the table-top we had cleared before they arrived. I will be breezy and cool and tell him what I want out of this display so he can get to work and I can get back to my workbench.

Clearing my throat as I walk past Desi and Tate, I square my shoulders as I walk towards Seb.

"Desi, let's discuss this job with them and let them get to it, I'm sure they have a busy schedule." I say tightly.

Desi's eyes flick to Tate, who is smiling at me and pulling his big body up to walk over towards Seb as well. Why are they both so big? Gah! It's like being surrounded by trees of muscles and I have to close my eyes for a second to calm my nervous body.

Desi puts her arm around me and we both walk closer to where the men are standing. Seb is still glaring at the tools like they have insulted him personally, and Tate claps him on the shoulder, redirecting his attention. His eyes snap to me and he inhales sharply. Then his shoulders drop and he shakes his head as if clearing it. Oh my Gods, he is so fucking weird. What does it say about me that I am still super into him?

I take a step back and clear my throat again.

Desi chirps in and starts to explain what we want out of the display. How we picture the light coming through and what we plan to set up on this side of the store so that the men can share our vision. She is smooth and warm and calm and with every word she speaks, I feel frizzier and sharper. Like I have to balance out her chill with my own frenetic energy.

Desi and Tate do all the talking. Shocker! Seb pulls out a small notebook and dutifully jots down the details of what Desi is saying, every once and a while glancing at me from under his eyebrows and I rip my gaze away every time. If I was wearing a sweater with a hood I would be hiding in it right now. Just bury my head in the sand like a very mature and put together ostrich and be done with my day.

Oh Lords above, this is going to be a long couple of weeks.

Chapter 8

Seb

After scenting her when she came back into the room, I know she isn't aroused anymore. That is both a huge relief and also incredibly disappointing. My Wolf is not impressed with my behaviour. He is pacing inside of me, bristling at my stupidity. He knows that she had wanted us, and I had managed to fuck it up, yet again. She smelled too good. I had felt delirious with it and I panicked. In my haste to give her space before my Wolf did something deranged, like decide that now was the time to claim her or expose us, I ran away. I turned tail and hot-footed it away from her as fast as I could go. Jesus fuck I'm an idiot. She must think I am a lost cause. Why would she be interested in a guy who can't manage to complete a single sentence in her presence without making it weird. Every time I get around her I turn into a gaping carp or worse, a grunting caveman.

But my Wolf won't give up on her. Hell, I'm not going to give up on her, I honestly don't think I can. But I don't have the smooth charm that Tate does. All I do is make gruff conversation at best before I feel my Wolf getting involved and then, in classic Seb style, make it awkward.

But she *had* been aroused before, so that tells me that I have a chance to prove to her that I can be a decent mate. That I can woo her? Should I woo her? How the hell will I do that?

I should woo her.

She is watching me now. While Desi describes to Tate and me what they want us to build for them, she watches me. As Desi talks, I'm taking notes, jotting numbers down based on the space. I get a picture in my mind of what they'd like and I draw quick sketches. Cora glances away whenever I look up at her. Like she doesn't want me to catch her watching me. Does she feel this pull between us too? I take deep breaths to control my Wolf. To control myself. Every time I do, I inhale the delicious scent that is all her, and my Wolf is soothed just knowing that she is near. I realize I am sad sacking, my shoulders and head low, and I straighten my spine. I'm a big guy and often I try to appear smaller to the humans around me. Something about a really big man unsettles people sometimes so I try to make myself seem smaller. To blend in.

But something has shifted now. I don't want to make myself small. I want to be myself.

I want Cora to see me, really see me, for who I really am. My size and strength are assets to a mate. I stretch my muscles subtly, rolling my shoulders back gradually. Standing as tall as I actually am and not shrinking from myself.

Tate and Desi are still talking about the job, and I look back over at Cora. She is staring at me, her delicate mouth slightly parted.

My Wolf chuffs in my chest and preens for her. I can

feel the rumble of his pleasure start in my ribs and work its way up my throat.

She slowly blinks, like she is waking up from a trance, and clears her throat.

I hold her gaze and shift on my feet slightly so I am facing her. I take her in, soaking up her features while she is still mesmerized by me. Just the fact that she hasn't broken eye contact already and her lips are slightly parted tells me that she is a little lost in this moment. Like I am.

I inhale deeply and can scent her arousal again. The growling in my chest grows. Cora blinks again and shakes her head just a little, as if to clear it, and she narrows her eyes.

"Are you hungry?" She asks me.

Tate glances over at me with a smirk and I clear my throat, trying to get a grip on my Wolf.

"Uh, what?" Genius conversationalist over here.

"Is that your stomach growling? Do you need to eat?" She asks.

I hear Tate snicker, and he turns Desi around subtly to walk them away from Cora and I. My wingman is on point even though I'm a bumbling idiot. Once they are far enough away that I know that Desi won't hear our conversation, even though Tate definitely still will, I turn my attention back to Cora.

"I could eat."

She frowns at me a little more and crosses her arms over her chest. The motion pushes her breasts together under her shirt and I can see the slight swells above the top button. She wears these soft collared shirts all the time with the collar popped and it is distractingly attractive. The top buttons are always undone and her soft skin flashes as she moves.

I want to see her in one of my flannels. My Wolf wants

to see that too, his pleased grumble increasing at the thought.

She is still frowning at me, like she's debating the pros and cons of something important, and she finally speaks again.

"Should you eat then? Would you like to grab something from the cafe next door?" she asks. Her tone is flat, like she is trying to sound nonchalant.

Does she want to come with me? Is she asking me to eat with her??

Blinking as I take a small step towards her, I watch her reaction. She holds her ground and tilts her head up slightly to keep looking at my face.

"Are you… would you like to come with me?" I ask her quietly.

She inhales sharply, like she wasn't expecting me to ask, and I want to shrink away from her. I've misread the situation. My eagerness to be close to her and move forward with her is blinding me to what's really happening. I shouldn't have asked, of course she doesn't want to go get lunch with me.

"Yes, I would." she whispers.

Chapter 9

Cora

"Yes, I would." I whisper, watching him, seeing him take deep breaths as he gazes at me. Because that's absolutely what he is doing. His eyes are locked on mine and I am getting dizzy.

Listening to his deep breaths, I close my eyes to get my racing heart under control.

Seb clears his throat and shifts a step back from me.

"Great, that's great." He says quietly. His voice is deep and low, full of gravel. It's like we have stepped into a bubble of time, just the two of us, and all the sights and sounds around us are hushed. It's only us.

Touch me, I think to myself; oh Gods, I want him to reach out and touch me. I realize I am leaning in towards him and his eyes widen when he notices it too. He steps back into my space and I huff out a breath that I hadn't realized I was holding. His heat pushes against me, sending my skin into a tizzy of sensation, a flare of tingling sparks races across my shoulders and down my spine.

Gah, he is so dreamy. His scruffy hair looks like he's been raking his hands through it and it stands up all over the place. He has a smudge of graphite along his temple where he's tucked his flat carpenter's pencil behind his ear. I want to run my hands through his hair and see if it's as soft as I have been imagining. Smooth it out a bit with my fingers. But just a bit. I realize that I like him looking dishevelled. Like he is a storm of movement and energy moving through the world.

Hells bells, I have it baaaad.

I clear my throat again and rock back on my heels.

"Ok, great, um. I guess we should go then?" I say. Still staring him in the eyes. His mouth slowly crooks up on one side, a half-grin that I have never seen before, and I DIE. Holy crap, he is just so fucking cute, somehow more attractive than usual, and my heart is racing and I can feel my body clenching in sudden need. Deep breath Cora, get a hold of yourself! He inhales deeply and then chuffs out a sudden breath, his eyes growing dark, hungry. Oh, what the hell is this sorcery? What is he doing with his eyes? What IS THIS?

He's into you, a little voice in my head sings. He's into you and those eyes are fucking you right now. Birds and squirrels are singing all around me and I can feel the tips of my fingers getting hot and tingly.

Oh Shit. Abort mission! All power to rear engines, warp speed Mr. Sulu!

"Ah, ok awesome so uh, let's go grab some lunch then, I'll see what Desi wants to eat, do you want to see about what Tate wants to eat? I'm going to just go ask Desi what she wants to eat!" I blurt out, my voice high, foolishly and belatedly realizing that my magic has been pushing at me and I wasn't noticing because of Seb's stormy sex eyes, letting myself get lost in the dreamy depths like a love-struck teenager.

I scramble to the front door and grab Desi's arm as I swing past.

"Can I talk to you real quick, just for a second? I need to ask you about food things right now!"

She looks at me in bewilderment, because why on earth wouldn't she. I'm suddenly a rambling idiot and Tate is looking at me now too and my ears are getting hot and I can feel my hair start to gently move away from my head like there is a breeze. Inside our shop.

Desi catches on that my magic is up to some tricks, looking for an escape route from the frantic energy tumbling around my body right now.

"Oh, I love food things!" Desi exclaims brightly, shooting a megawatt smile at Tate, while she follows me quickly into the fresh air.

We scurry towards our side alley, along the left-hand side of the building, where we have a covered courtyard separate from the sidewalk traffic. Slamming the wrought iron gate behind us, Desi swirls around to face me and grabs me by the shoulders.

"Deep slow breaths, Baby Girl, you've got this." She soothes me. She is breathing deep and slow, right along with me and it helps. Just like it always does when my magic gets the better of me and I start to panic.

"You're pulling those hot feelings back up your arms, and the heat is settling in your belly. Feel it settle in, Honey." She coaxes me as I visualize the breeze that I am creating being gently sucked back into my body with every breath I take in. I've been using this breathing technique since we were preteens, my mom had taught us. The months leading up to my first period were a hellscape of burnt t-shirts and broken pottery. My magic pushing to get free and my desperate attempts to contain it at every turn. Once Desi had figured out that I responded well with a coach, she had stepped up like the angel she is and learned the tricks right alongside me. I fidget with my ring: a simple silver band that mom had given me years ago. Engraved on the inside with the latin words 'Custodio Serenitatem', it was a tangible reminder to guard my magic with peace. I often feel like my magic is fighting to get out of me and I fiercely hold it in check, a regular battle of wills with myself. It's exhausting, but the alternative is unbearable.

Slowly, my breathing and thrumming energy stills and calms. I am a pillar of peace. I am a bubbling spring. I am a sloth napping in the jungle.

"There you go, Babe, ooh Honey Cruller, you are so good at that! I know you were panicking there for a hot minute, but you totally had that in the bag!" Desi's eternal optimism is a balm to my nerves right now and I pull her into me for a fierce hug.

"Thank you, Des." I huff into her ear. "That felt like a close one."

She nods her head, smiling confidently at me. "It was pretty close, what happened back there?"

I shake my hands out at my sides, getting the last stray bits of magic out of my system as I look at her.

Taking a breath, I confess.

"He gave me sex eyes and I liked it. And then I realized my magic was getting sneaky and I panicked. So I ran away."

"Yeah, you sure did!" Although, since she said it with a smile and a waggle of her eyebrows I can't get too snarly with her.

Also, it was true. I totally ran away. I pulled a Seb, because that's usually what he does.

Wait.

He usually ran away from *me*. In a weird, I've got to get the heck out of dodge sort of way.

"Desi." I breathe.

"Yeah, Babe?" She's calmly watching me, waiting for me to work it out.

"Does Seb have magic too? Could that be why he's always freaking out and running away from me?" I really hope that he does, because the idea of him running away just because of me doesn't sit very well in my gut. It stirs up a lot of unpleasantness that I prefer to keep squashed down viciously in my subconscious. It reminds me that I am going to push him away, just like I pushed my dad away. That I need to control my magic to keep people. I like Seb, as much as we are awkward as hell around each other, I think that maybe there could be something there. I just need to hide what I am.

Maybe it's just romantic wishful thinking on my part. But I like him, and I feel a warm tug in my chest whenever I think about him.

Chapter 10

Seb

"Are you going to ask me about lunch, big brother?" Tate asks me.

I realize with a start that I have been staring at the front door since the women rushed out.

She ran away this time.

Why have our roles suddenly reversed?

"Huh?" I slowly turn my head towards him, remembering that he just said something.

"Dude, the girls went outside to talk about 'lunch'," Tate smirks, making the quotation hand signal and raising his eyebrows at me.

"What happened back there?" He asks, while I continue to just stare at him. I feel bewildered. What happened just now? I let my thoughts drift over the last few moments. Our exchange had felt charged with electricity, fraught with a deeper tension than usual. I have kept myself apart from her in the past, keeping my yearning Wolf as far from her canny, dark eyes as I could while getting as close as I dared. The pull of the Mate Bond didn't allow me to create too much distance between us, but the knowledge that I was an alpha werewolf and that she had no idea of just how much that meant between us ensured that I fought the pull for her sake. She deserved to have a choice. And why would she choose me?

But this time, everything feels different. She held my gaze and her cheeks had flushed prettily, her midnight eyes pulling me into their depths and her heartbeat thrumming in time with mine. The way that her scent had shifted to one of smokey heat drove my Wolf wild with satisfaction. She had gasped when I stepped into her space, a soft sound escaping her lips that had shot directly to the base of my spine. I couldn't have moved away from her if I wanted to. She held me trapped happily in her gaze. Until she bolted. The warmth that had crept over me in those moments together had fled with her, leaving me chilled.

I realize that my fists are clenched tight and I take a shuddering breath, shaking my hands out.

"We, we were talking to each other…" I start.

"With real words?" Tate cajoles, bumping my shoulder with his.

I snort, glaring at him.

"Yes asshole, with real words."

I don't tell him about her getting aroused. About how fucking delicious she smells and how there is an undeniable pull between us. That she has to be feeling something too. That is my information. Just for me.

"I thought that she was… but then she bolted." I end with, stiffly. I suspect that Tate probably knows that she is attracted to me. His nose is as good as mine. He's aware that my Wolf has acknowledged that she's ours. But he also knows that I am a fuckwit and have messed up nearly every interaction that she and I have ever had.

Running my fingers through my hair I knock the flat pencil out from behind my ear. I had forgotten that it was there. I had forgotten that we are here for a job and that today is only the first day of many in the coming weeks that I will spend so close to Cora.

I can be patient. My Wolf is happy to lay down a prolonged hunt. Shit, we've already been essentially stalking her for the last year since we met them at the market that day. He isn't content to wait forever, but now that we know she is feeling something too, my Wolf is feeling oddly satisfied. Like playing the long game is always what he expected.

But what is she feeling? Besides being obviously attracted to me, a fact that makes my chest swell and my cheeks flush, thinking about her sweet, smokey scent.

But she bolted. So maybe, maybe she is fighting that attraction?

I admit to myself with chagrin that I haven't really given her a reason not to fight it.

I've been surly, grumpy and honestly, when I think about my actions around her, I realize I have essentially been glowering at her and dashing away like a fool for the last year.

It is certainly not my intention to be a fucking weirdo every time I see her. But my Wolf is a persistent bastard when it comes to her and the growling starts in my chest and I seize up and jet.

Women just love that.

I want to understand what makes her who she is. I already know that my Wolf is obsessed with her, hell I am too. She's clever and beautiful and I have watched her interact with the other locals so I know that she is well respected here. Whatever it is that she's holding close, I want to know it. Know her.

I clear my throat and look over at Tate. He waits patiently, his good nature always looking toward the bright side of every situation. He doesn't sweat about flirting with Desi. They have a friendly, teasing banter that's annoying as fuck, but I am aware enough to recognize that I'm jealous of his easy connection to people. His eternal optimism sometimes grates on my rough edges, but I am always glad that he can be who he is.

"Let's figure out lunch and draw up some preliminary sketches for their display. I've got some ideas that I think they will like." I say.

"I bet you do," he replies. "Alright, let's get started"

Chapter 11

Cora

Sundays are my favourite.

Quiet mornings spent reflecting on the week ahead, moving slowly through the world with a cup of something warm, getting my hands into a bowl of herbs. Losing myself in the small magics of spell casting and creation, even if it's just mixing a batch of fresh tea, like I am today. I let my mind wander while I work through the familiar ritual of blending blossoms and leaves. Pulling the jars down from my shelves, grounding myself in the beautiful monotony of a comforting task.

This past week has been a blur of heightened emotions, the familiar routine of a busy work schedule and many, many stolen glances.

Seb and Tate have turned out to be a surprisingly lovely addition to our team here at the shop. They are doing the majority of the building in their studio across town, but pop in daily with questions or to re-measure something, and in Tate's case, shamelessly flirt with Desi.

That man is pure positivity and charm, and I am happy for Desi, since she seems to be enjoying the attention.

Seb is less weird than usual too. He seems to be able to drop his guard a little bit around me lately and it has made our interactions less like a cringe-worthy teen angst fest and more like an awkward, slightly older, young adult angst fest. But it feels like progress and since I am equally to blame for the stilted wariness around each other, I'm not one to judge.

Seb has been calmer, more sure of himself since that morning last week in the shop. That morning I had run away from him, my magic had nearly escaped my rigid control because I had found myself getting a little bit lost in his gaze. It didn't help that I had wanted to get lost in it. And then, when the way he had been looking at me changed? When his eyes turned dark and hungry? Holy hot flash Batman, I shiver every time I think about it.

Because, when I am honest with myself, I want to push my body into his and lick his neck and generally get freaky all over him. Which is out of character for me. But other than being surprised by my wanton reaction to him, I'm pretty ok with it.

I'm expecting Seb in the shop today. He had gruffly mentioned to me the previous evening that he was scheduled to have the display finished in a week, but he wanted to bring a section of it into the space and make sure things were lining up the way he wanted.

Once Desi and I had given them our go-ahead with some of the beautiful sketches they had shown us, we felt confident in their skills and had let them get to it. I am a bit type A sometimes when it comes to my work, but since seeing the drawings that Seb made of the corner of the shop with the new display in it, I feel confident that we are in good hands. Big, calloused hands with blunt fingers. Hands that I imagine can palm my ass as he pulls my hips into his body, pressing my needy core against his tight, jean-clad lap. Hands that can scratch my shoulders and pinch my tight nipples and pull my hair and…

"Hey my beautiful Cupcake, what are you doing to that cardamom?" Desi trills at me, her voice close behind me.

"WHAT? Huh?! Nothing!" I shriek, dropping the little handful of spice pods I was squeezing the life out of and spinning around to hide my flaming cheeks from my best friend.

Pulling a ragged breath into my lungs and shaking my hands out, I pull my shoulders back and blink at Desi, who had walked up behind me like a regular person and not a stealth ninja. I realize belatedly that she had been asking me something as she walked over, but I was so lost in my deliciously dirty daydream about Seb and his huge, hot hands that I completely missed all of it. Clearing my throat and trying for a casual tone, my voice actually comes out high and squeaky. "Ah, would you repeat that?"

Desi chuckles at me and slips in next to me for a side hug.

"I was asking if you had seen the email from Tate that was sent this morning?"

"Oh? No, I haven't been on the computer yet. I came straight back here to mix up a fresh batch of the Spiced Tea blend when I came in."

"Mmm-hmmm." she hums.

"It looks like you might have to start another batch, Honey Bee." She says softly, pointedly glancing at the big glass bowl in front of me.

Huh?

I look down and groan out loud.

"Oh, for fucks sake!" I drop my face into my palm.

My Spiced Tea blend is looking decidedly worse for wear. In my sultry daydreaming stupor, I mistook oregano for lavender, and the whole batch smells like pasta sauce with a chai chaser.

"Take a breather, BabyRuth." Desi consoles me, grinning. "It happens to the best of us."

I groan again as I heft the big bowl out to the back door to dump into the compost. We have a little herb garden in our private courtyard behind the store and my little green bin is tucked in next to tidy rows of calendula plants.

Rubbing my hands together as I come back into the workroom, I ask Desi about the email.

"Is everything ok? What did Tate say in the message?"

"Oh, he said that things were coming along nicely and that they were on schedule. But he had a couple of questions about hardware. They found a wholesaler who was closing up their business and had gotten their big, hot hands on some vintage knobs that we might like."

She practically purrs that last sentence at me.

"Ohmygods Desi, did you hear my fantasy just now?" I hiss at her.

"You were projecting pretty loud there, SweetTart and it was deliciously not safe for work. Lucky for you, we are boss babes." She smiles at me. Desi has no shame, and I am constantly mortified. I groan out loud again. I don't think my cheeks can get any hotter and I'm already focusing on the tingles buzzing in my fingertips. I reach into my top drawer for a lavender oil roll-on and liberally anoint my neck and wrists. Breathing in the calming scent, I glare at her. She just laughs in her beautiful way and bumps her hip with mine.

"Don't be embarrassed Lovey, I plan to do a lot worse

to Tate when I get my grabby hands on him. Mmmm that man revs my engine!"

I bark a sharp laugh and let my embarrassment slide down my arms. I am a healthy grown-up lady person and I can own my sexual fantasies damn it!

"Seb is on his way over now." Desi says softly.

I trip over my own feet in the doorway as I turn around so quickly that I ram my shoulder into the frame.

"RIGHT NOW?" I practically holler and Desi beams at me while I rub my arm.

"Yep, should be here any minute."

Chapter 12

Seb

I pull the van up to Cora's shop's back alley. She and Desi have a courtyard in the back of the shop filled with plants and solar lights. I imagine them lounging back there in the summer after a day in the shop and smile to myself. They have a great little setup here.

Tate and I are still staying with Aunt Jett, although it's more like we rent the carriage house at this point. Uncle Frank had a big workshop that he had built years ago, presumably to finish up as a B&B. But ultimately it never got used for anything other than Uncle Frank's man cave. Aunt Jett had basically handed the keys over to us shortly after we moved to town. I think that she wanted us close because we would be helpful around the property and she was a bit lonely in her dotage. But she didn't actually want us inside her house because we are two huge, nearly thirty-year-old men with all of the mess that comes with us. Honestly, I don't think we are that bad. Considering how much travelling we've been doing in the last few years, we don't have a lot of stuff. Other than the clothes we brought with us, and a few small souvenirs picked up along the way, we are pretty self-contained. Tate has a burgeoning shoe collection started now that we have settled in town, and I've been fixing up Frank's old tools. But otherwise, we only use the stuff already in the apartment. It's mostly cast-off furniture from the main house and some of the wood pieces that Uncle Frank had built over the years. That being said, Jett definitely keeps her space considerably tidier than Tate and I keep ours. Even with all the chickens that have moved insolently into the house proper.

Scanning my eyes over the little courtyard as I enter, I notice with a smile that Cora and Desi lean more towards Aunt Jett's end of the scale in the cleanliness department. The plants are neatly lined up in tidy boxes and the brick pathway is swept clean. Since we are heading into October and the leaves are steadily falling, one of the women must have swept back here recently.

I unlock the van's back gate and start pulling my tools out, stacking them by the shop's back door. I can hear the soft mumble of voices inside, likely Cora and Desi, since this door leads to the back storage room and they are closed on Sundays.

I hear Cora clearly then, she exclaims something with a sharp voice and I pause.

I don't want to eavesdrop but my Wolf is pacing in my chest, intent on getting closer to her. Listening in on their conversation is more than I want to do, however. I will never gain her trust if I am caught with my ear to the door, so I clear my throat loudly and make a little more noise than strictly necessary getting the last box of tools next to the door. I still have to grab the main piece of the display we have built for them, but I want to get the tools inside and out of the way before hauling the heavy piece out of the van.

I knock on the door, making sure to keep making as much noise as possible, and then slowly push it open with my hip, picking up a heavy box of tools as I enter. Someone scrabbles away from the backroom and I look up to see Desi grinning at me like the cat that got the cream.

"Hey Seb!" she greets me. She is wearing a long crocheted cardigan thing over a long dress and she looks a bit like an elf. A self-satisfied elf? Why is she looking at me like that?

"Hey Desi, I've got the main piece of the display in the van. I'm just going to bring some tools in first." I say quietly.

"Awesome, thank you Seb, I have a few things I need to see to in the office upstairs, but Cora is in the shop." She waves to me over her shoulder as she heads upstairs and I watch her go, feeling puzzled.

Her eye contact felt pointed like she was trying to tell me something or like she knows something. Hells if I know what she is trying to communicate though, her wide eyes and smirking mouth don't give me enough to go on.

Desi is weird.

I shake my head; worrying about the complexities of women isn't going to get this job done, and likely won't help me figure out what Desi was attempting to convey to me. So I grab my tools and bring them into the front shop area.

Cora is there, looking flushed and utterly gorgeous as usual. Her pink hair is tied up in a messy bun at the top of her head, and there are wispy tendrils floating around her face. She is looking at me with an odd expression that I can't quite place. I can hear her heartbeat from here, fast and fluttery like a bird. Her dark eyes move over my body in a way that feels brazen, something that I have never felt her do before. I can feel her eyes on my skin like a touch, whispering under my clothes and sending my Wolf into a tailspin of giddy desire. I realize that I am staring at her and blink to break the spell.

"Morning." I mutter, crouching to put the box of tools down. She blinks at me then, her eyes locked onto my hands on the box, and then she shivers like she is cold.

"Good morning, Seb." She replies. Her voice is husky this morning. My Wolf ripples under my skin hearing her say my name. I can feel him padding towards the surface and I clench my fists at my sides, breathing deeply to give myself a moment to reign him in.

"I, uh, I've got another load of tools to bring in and then I'll grab the finished display." I start to turn to grab the tools when Cora's voice stops me.

"Are you done already? I thought it would be a little longer."

Is that disappointment I hear? A surge of pleasure flows down my back and I nearly lose my grip on my Wolf.

"Oh, uh no, this is just the first piece. I want to make sure that it fits with the space before starting the second part." I say.

"Great! Good, okay!" She says, a little breathless. The relief in her tone makes me want to puff up my chest and preen like a pretty idiot.

"Cool." I reply.

"Are you ok today?" I have to ask her, desperately hoping for the answer I want to hear. As much as I want her to have suddenly decided that she is attracted to me, her behaviour is out of character and if it's because she isn't feeling well, my Wolf wants to take care of her.

"Me? Oh yeah, super cool. Suuuper, super cool. Yep, fine. Totally fine." She squeaks in response, her cheeks reddening further. I tilt my head at her, watching her closely. She is radiating embarrassment. I can't think of why she might be feeling that way, long having lost the ability to view her as anything other than perfection. And I have such a tight rein on my Wolf that I can't scent her to be sure. Letting him get closer to the surface when Cora is so close to me is a recipe for disaster. I haven't shifted in a few days and he is ready to burst out of me now that he knows she is right here, watching us in a new way. Cora isn't usually so unhinged, but I'm not sure if she wants me to be the one to help her feel better. So I nod at her and go back out to the van to bring the finished piece in.

Chapter 13

Cora

Calm the fuck down you twitterpated ninny, CALM DOWN!

I 'm positively simmering in nerves. Logically I know that Seb can't hear my thoughts and that there is no way that he will know that I was imagining him doing dirty, *dirty* things to my body while I was at work, mere moments before he walked into said workplace. But my bonkers lizard brain is not having any of that. No logic for her! I am trembling all over and I can feel my hair moving around my head.

Get a grip on yourself woman! I run into the bathroom and lock the door behind me. I just need a few minutes to bring my energy down and face reality like a reasonable witch. I can be reasonable. I can, Gods dammit.

My hands are still shaking and I look at myself in the mirror. The face looking back at me is wild and glossy-eyed, cheeks flushed so much that the redness has travelled and spread across new facial territory into full face cartography, and I actually cringe when I take in my hair. Oh

Gods, it's all over the damned place. No wonder Seb was looking at me like he was, I look deranged! I run the cold water and splash some over my hot cheeks, and stand still just breathing and staring at myself for a minute.

I can do this.

Be normal.

Contain your bloody magic and get out there and be a badass boss bitch.

I focus on my energy, using another visualization technique from my youth, and imagine a ball of bright blue energy swirling with orange. I imagine the orange swirls getting smaller and smaller until there's just a blue bubble. Then I take a deep, slow breath in and imagine the blue ball getting smaller and smaller until I can hold it in my hand.

I reach out and take the now golf ball-sized orb of glittering energy out of the air in my mind's eye and gently close my fist around it. It sinks into my skin and I feel it settle into my core, liquid and cool as it moves through me. I take another deep breath and slowly blink my eyes open. I look at myself in the mirror, hoping for a full return to normal. Or at least as normal as I usually look. My hair is no longer swirling around my head, and my eyes look less wild.

Crisis averted!

I relax my shoulders and take my hair out from its messy bun. It feels really good to let it down so I take a moment to run my fingers through it and get the tangles out. I almost never wear it loose. Ever since I accidentally spelled it pink, it felt like a social road flare. Look at the witch! Look at what she did. She can't control her magic! Boo hiss, social pitch forkery blah blah blah. I know, deep down, that it's ridiculous, no one is pointing at me and hissing. This goofy town is so welcoming and obnoxiously inclusive that even if I was caught traipsing down main street buck naked, the worst I would get is some hairy eyeballs. More likely than not, someone would assume that I was making my way to a nude moon ritual or something and use the town's community Facebook group to call in reinforcements. Jett would probably bring pie.

I run my hands through my hair repeatedly, letting my scalp relax from being pulled tight into my top knot for so long, and rub circles along my temporal line.

After a minute, I feel settled and calm, and I gently weave my hair into a braid down one side. It is one thing to enjoy the feeling of having my hair down and loose. But it is quite another to leave it down around Seb and run the risk of my magic flaring up again and having it float around my head like I'm a mermaid underwater.

Nothing screams totally normal like swirling, zero-gravity hair.

I straighten my shoulders and open the bathroom door. The hallway is clear and I can hear Seb in the front room moving things around. I walk over in that direction and stop in my tracks when I see him. He's facing away from me, carefully moving some of our inventory out of the way. His big shoulders are hunched over a little and I watch him pause to sniff one of my tea blends.

I smile a little at the sight. He is just so *brawny*. All hulking muscles and long, lean legs. Watching him hold the little tin so gently to his nose is adorable.

I clear my throat and he stiffens, turning to look over his shoulder at me. He looks a little sheepish, and I smile again.

"Do you drink tea?" I ask him, as I walk closer to where he is standing. He gingerly holds the small tin in his big hands as he turns around to face me.

"Yeah," He replies. "Aunt Jett has a whole collection

that she likes to share with Tate and I. This one smells really good. Is that coriander in there?"

Surprised that he caught that scent, I raise my eyebrows as I reply, "It is; you've got a good nose."

He huffs out a small laugh and puts the tea sample tin back on the shelf.

"I hope you don't mind that I started moving things around. I just wanted to get the space cleared out a little bit more."

"Not at all," I reply. "I actually meant to move more of this out of here before you arrived, so I'll help now."

I move over to him a little bit and he steps back. I glance up at him, worried that I'm invading his personal space, but his expression isn't telling me that he wants to get away from me. This time anyway. He takes a breath in, holds it for a second, and then lets it out slowly. Like he was counting to five in his head.

I raise one of my brows at him and he shrugs.

Our non-verbal communication is on point it seems, and we both get to work moving the tea display over and wrapping up a selection of mugs that my potter friend had dropped off the day before. We work quietly, neither of us interested in breaking the comfortable silence that we've never really had before.

Chapter 14

Seb

She's changed her hair.

I notice it as soon as I turn around. She had escaped into the bathroom while I finished carrying the dismantled display pieces into the shop. I heard the water running and her quick breathing through the door when I had walked past it, so I got myself started in the shop moving some of the stuff around.

They carry a nice selection of handmade things here. I haven't really spent a lot of time in their store before, because being surrounded by her scent seemed like it would have been a lesson in self-torture, it would have driven me wild. No pun intended. Although I'm surrounded by her scent now and have been all week. I haven't lost myself to my Wolf's desires. He is calm right now; perhaps I've been avoiding coming in here for no reason?

I'm checking out the tea samples when I hear her steps behind me. She doesn't come all the way into the room, so

I pretend that I don't know exactly where she is for a minute. Letting her nearness wash over me. Her scent is always intoxicating, sweet and a little smokey, like the amber I can smell in some of the smudge bundles they have in the shop.

But the more time I spend with her, the more I am starting to believe that my lovely Mate may be more than she seems. Over this past week, I have had more opportunities to get closer to her, and there is an undercurrent to her scent I never noticed before. It's a little bit wild, like a summer storm, and it makes me want to dig deeper into her true nature. But I want her to be the one to tell me because she trusts me. The irony is not lost on me. I'm keeping my Wolf a secret from her too, but it's different. Werewolves are not always the most accepted in the magical community, there are so few of us, and we keep to our packs for the most part. Not to mention some of the ridiculous lore that humans have spread about us over the centuries, leaving a dark stain on our reputation. Whatever she is can't possibly be dangerous, she's too delicate to be a threat. So I tuck that information away for now and just revel in her nearness. With my Wolf feeling calm, sensing that her energy is not as frantic as before, I let him a little closer to the surface. He chuffs softly with contentment to be near her.

She clears her throat behind me, I think to let me know that she is there. Like I don't know where she is all the time. But I play along, straightening my shoulders and glancing at her over my shoulder. She smiles and my Wolf preens inside of me.

"Do you drink tea?" She asks as she walks closer to me. I greedily take her in as she walks closer. Her hair is now woven over one shoulder in a slightly messy braid, the strands that frame her face are smooth. Her eyes are bright and I blink to keep myself from getting lost in them.

We talk quietly about Aunt Jett and her tea collection and then we work silently together for a little while, moving things around and packing up some delicate mugs that are close to where I will be working.

At one point she raises an eyebrow, a question in her eyes. This new comfort between us is a gift, one I don't want to reject by ruining the moment. So I just shrug and we continue working together in comfortable silence.

She is close to me, the space doesn't really allow us to get too far away from each other, and I have to close my eyes when her sweet scent flows into my lungs. My Wolf is pleased as fucking punch about it. She's crouching next to me, packing up little tins of tea into a box that I had grabbed for her from the back room earlier, and I pause to really take her scent in. I lean a little closer to her. Her back is turned to me, her focus intent on her task until she suddenly stiffens. She whips her head around and pins me in place with her glare.

"Did you just sniff me?" She asks, her eyes wide as she leans back from me.

"Uh?!" I back-pedal, giving her space, "I um, yes? Your… shampoo smells nice and I ah, may have sniffed your hair?" I am cringing, oh fuck, I am such a guilty-looking asshole!

I straighten. I cough to clear my throat.

"Sorry, that was weird and I am really sorry Cora."

She is frowning at me, her brilliant eyes calculating behind her lashes and I shove my hands into my pockets and hunch my shoulders, attempting to look non threatening. As non threatening as a six and a half foot tall bloody werewolf can be at least.

She considers me for a long moment and then blinks, a delicate furrow between her brows.

"It's an amber vanilla blend I make," she says quietly. She turns back to her tea tins and… lets me off the hook? Not looking this gift horse in the mouth, I step away from her and continue to clear the space for the new display. We work for another half hour or so, and then she offers to grab us sandwiches from the cafe a few doors down.

After she leaves I move the pieces of the new display into place and put it all together so it will be ready for her when she comes back. I want her to feel pleased with the progress and forget all about my olfactory faux pas.

Chapter 15

Cora

I barely hold my flustered limbic system under control while I continue to work next to Seb after The Sniff Incident. Sweet baby Jesus in a bunny suit. I could feel the heat of him behind me, hyper-aware of where his body was in context to mine while we worked together. I was suppressing the hell out of my reactions to him all morning! And then the sexy fucker sidled right in and *sniffed me.* Good gravy. And then he blushed and stammered adorably. Making him impossibly cuter, and then, *THEN*, the way his deep voice said my name made my knees feel wobbly and my needy lady parts sing like a gospel choir. I shake my head and try to let the memories flow over me. Get it together woman!

My phone pings in my pocket, startling me out of my lusty tailspin. I pull it out of my pocket and snort when I see Desi's contact waiting for me to respond.

. . .

Desi: Tell me everything

Cora: What are you even talking about?

Desi: TELL ME EVERYTHING. You need to talk this out.

I laugh, the sound a little strangled, but promptly reply.

Cora: Do you already know??

Desi: Spill it sister

Cora: OMG he is so nice and cute and sweet and his big arms and tight butt and he smells sooo goooood and we were packing up inventory and we had this nice comfy silence thing happening and then he SNIFFED MY HAIR

Desi: Yeah he did. Then what?

Cora: I called him on it

Desi: YES YOU DID! I love this part, keep going

Cora: DESI!

. . .

Desi: Cora

Cora:

Desi: UGH you are no fun sometimes! Fine! You called him on it and told him that it was your own blend and like a fucking boss you went right back to work and let him stew in his stewy juices!

Cora: Basically yes

Desi: I love you (heart eyes emoji face)

Cora: I love you too (heart emoji)

Desi: please grab me a vegan bowl while you are at the cafe. I am WILTING like a delicate flower up here.

Cora: (Laughing face emoji) Will do.

Cora: I need to get out to McLaren's Wood in the next week or so. There are a couple of herbs that will be ready to harvest soon and I want to get a

jump on some holiday blends. Wanna come with me for a moonlit forest adventure?

Desi: You know I do babe. I will soak up mama Moon's good juju while you dig in the dirt.

Now go get me that buddha bowl before I expire.

Cora: (eyeroll emoji face)

When I get back to the shop, I have probably been gone for about thirty minutes. In that time, Seb has set up the new display section and has managed to put some of the inventory back. He is… not great at merchandising, but the effort is charming. I find myself slowing my steps to take it all in. He's stacked some mugs on one of the new shelves along with some of my fresh tea blends and he's woven in some twinkly lights, obviously poached from another display section.

He turns around and sees me then. He shoots that half-grin my way and I swoon. I sigh like a teenager at a Harry Styles concert and butterflies throw a disco dance party in my stomach. Oh, this man. I squash my giddiness down to a more reasonable level as casually as I can.

I smile back at him, nearly restored to my full faculties, and lift the bag of treats from the bakery.

"I return victorious." I say, walking over to the beautiful new display cabinet that this hunky hulk has built for me. With his big, calloused, capable hands. *Stop it, Cora!*

I shake myself a little and put the sandwiches down on the counter. I take Desi's buddha bowl out of the paper bag and place it next to the sandwiches.

Desi herself saunters down the stairs as I take off my

coat and sling it haphazardly across the stool we keep behind the counter.

"Mmmm, thank you, Dearest." She croons to me and steps over to kiss me on the cheek as she grabs her lunch.

"You're welcome, Darling." I retort, my fake fancy accent strong. I notice that Seb is watching us be ridiculous together. He is still half-smiling at me and I blush as I realize that Desi and I have fallen into our silly habit of pretending to be an old married couple. Like Darling and Jim Dear from *The Lady and The Tramp*. It is an old game that we have played since high school, when it had felt like it would always be the two of us against the world. Desi's eyes sparkle as she looks between Seb and me, and I blush even more.

"Seb Honey, this display is stunning!" She coos at him, spinning around to wander over to it and take a closer look. I watch her gaze skim over the lines of the cabinet that he and Tate have built for us and the haphazard selection of our regular stock that he's put together on it to show us how it might look once the whole piece is done.

The whole setup is lovely. They have made us an incredible custom piece that fits into our shop like it's always been here. It's a light coloured hardwood with subtle grain lines, and they've used a live edge piece for the main tabletop. The organic edges are offset with the rest of the modern, clean design. It is effortlessly beautiful. Somehow the angles of the piece and the custom shelves that come up from behind the main level feel light and airy, while the whole piece so far looks comfortingly solid. Like it will sit in this corner of our shop forever.

Desi hums to herself and grabs her lunch from the counter as she floats past me.

"I've got more invoices upstairs that won't file themselves, Honey Girl. I'll take my bowl to go." She says cheerily. She briefly touches my arm on her way past and I look at her. Her arched eyebrow tells me that she expects to be upstairs for a while, making herself scarce and I press my lips together trying to hide my smile.

I look towards Seb then and realize that he is watching me. I had gotten a little lost in the craftsmanship of this tangible object that he had created with his hands, and my dirty gutter brain thinks again about what those hands could do to me. My heart rate increases, heat flooding my cheeks and my spine tingles with a rush of arousal that dances down to my core, pooling warmth between my thighs. Seb's eyes are on me the whole time, his hands fisted at his sides. I blush even harder then, as I watch his eyes go dark and his grin falls slowly from his face. No longer is he boyishly handsome and charming. Now he is a man, gazing at a woman, who is seeing her own desires reflected back at her.

I blink and softly clear my throat.

"It really is beautiful, Seb, thank you." I say to him, my voice cracking over the shape of his name. He flushes slightly and nods. He's silent, like maybe he doesn't trust himself to speak? I had taken a step towards him without realizing it and stop myself. I inhale a ragged breath, and press my lips together to try to reign myself in. I turn around to the counter and grab the sandwich I ordered for him.

"Hungry?" I ask him, aiming for lightness in my tone. I am pretty sure it comes out husky though as he furrows his brows a little, still watching me with his hot, glittering eyes.

"Very." He practically growls at me and my core floods with a rush of liquid heat.

I gasp softly, staring up at him while I hold the wrapped sandwiches in front of me.

"Um, me too." I whisper. *Whaaat is happening right now?*

Chapter 16

Seb

"Um, me too." she whispers in response.

Her wide eyes are locked on mine and I can feel her arousal swirling around me. I hold my fists clenched tight at my sides. I am barely holding my Wolf contained, he is prowling inside me just itching to get out. Our mate is right in front of us, watching us with hot eyes, her pupils dark pools. Her desire is clearly written over her delicate features, and my Wolf is practically howling in pleasure. The rushing of my pulse pounds in my ears, nearly drowning out all other senses. My blood feels too hot, my skin prickling with awareness and lust. But more than that, the yearning pull to wrap her up in my arms and push my nose into her tender neck feels overwhelming. I desperately want to feel her body soften against me, and the more I want it, the harder it is to resist that draw. I know that I need to defuse this. I need to calm the beast inside of me and take things slowly. Cora still doesn't know what I am, and until she does I can't make a move.

I gently clear my throat and take a step towards her.

She gasps softly then, a sound that I've never heard her make before, and I groan low in my throat. She blinks up at me, I step in so close to her now that she has to tilt her head back to look up at me and I feel like I am looming over her. Her lips are slightly parted, and her soft breaths are coming in pants that I inhale deep into myself. Taking in her sweet scent, I close my eyes and tuck it away in my mind. I will always have her scent locked inside me.

She is holding our lunch tightly in her hands between us and I softly run my hands down her forearms from her elbows to her wrists. She watches my face, unblinking the whole time, until I slide my fingers over her hands and gently take my sandwich from her. My fingers feel full of electricity and I feel a warm draft wash over me from behind her.

"Guh..." she whispers, her glassy eyes blinking, and she shakes her head slightly.

She inhales sharply and her body strings tight.

"Ooh! OK!" She squeaks and clutches her own wrapped sandwich to her breasts.

"Uh, LET'S EAT IN THE COURTYARD!" She yells, her voice high, and she quickly jumps and takes a step back from me, creating the illusion of space between us.

My Wolf is amused by her reaction. He can feel her attraction to us and chuffs in my chest. She waves a hand around her hair and stumbles around me holding her sandwich so tight that I wouldn't be surprised if it was crushed.

I watch her scurry away from me and give her time to get to the courtyard. If she is feeling anything like I am, she needs it. I need it. My Wolf is simmering just under my skin and I take some deep, slow breaths to get myself under more control. After counting to twenty, I slowly walk through the hallway towards the private courtyard.

Cora is sitting at the little table, her eyes screwed shut and her still wrapped sandwich in front of her. She is taking measured breaths and I stutter step to a halt, realizing that she looks like she is controlling herself just like I am. My thoughts drift back to my suspicions about her nature, perhaps she is controlling something inside her that she's not ready to share, her own metaphorical wolf inside. I like the idea that we have more in common somehow. There are more things on this earth than most people realize. My brother and I are *werewolves* for fuck's sakes. Who am I to throw stones?

So I give her the time she needs to get whatever she is dealing with under control.

It doesn't take her long. Another minute stretches past us and I take advantage of the opportunity to drink in the sight of her. She is so lovely. Her button-up shirt is a deep navy blue today and made out of something soft but thick, so the collar stands up like a jacket. She always rolls the sleeves to her elbows and I imagine her at her workbench, stirring a big bowl of herbs to make her fancy tea blends and getting her soft hands into the mix.

Her hair is still braided over one shoulder and the shorter pieces around her face are floating in the soft breeze dancing around the courtyard.

The air stills as I watch her and she relaxes her posture just before opening her eyes.

She glances up at me and startles.

"Oh Seb, hey." Her voice is soft, steady.

"Can I sit with you while we eat?" I ask her. Not moving into the little space in case she needs more time.

"Yeah, sure." She scoots her chair over a little bit to make room for my longer legs.

I set myself down across from her and unwrap the sandwich she bought for me.

She watches me quietly for a minute before unwrapping her own, and we eat together in a little patch of sunlight. My Wolf settles inside me, curling up in contentment to have our Mate so close and comfortable next to us. This moment feels so good, the first time we have really just been settled together, and I want it to never end.

Chapter 17

Cora

"Girlfriend, you've got it baaaad." Desi sings to me later that night.

I really do. Seb and I had spent the rest of the day together in the shop. We worked together in comfortable silence for parts of the day, and we also enjoyed quiet conversations. He is charming and funny once he gets past communicating in only grunts and head nods.

I like him. A lot. And based on the looks he tossed my way all afternoon, and the way he found little ways to get close to me and touch me? I am confident in my assumption that he likes me too. I mean, nearly a year of longing glances and stolen looks has to amount to some kind of feelings from both of us, right?

"I really do." I say to Desi, looking up from the spreadsheet of account orders I am tracking for the store. I haven't actually tracked anything yet. I have however replayed a few moments from my afternoon with Seb like a movie highlight reel. Over and over again I replayed him brushing his shoulder against mine when we were restringing the twinkly lights he had poached earlier. And that moment by the counter when he had run his hands from my elbows to my wrists before gently taking his sandwich. Holy shit, I am *still* tingling from that one. I needed to escape after that. My fingers were steaming and I could feel the wind coursing through me. It was only a matter of time before my hair started floating, so I had bolted.

But he hadn't seemed spooked. After all the times over the last year when I had glared or snarled or generally been weird AF around him, he had stuck around today.

His weirdness seems to be settling too. Which is… really nice. Maybe we are both just terrible communicators and socially awkward and we just needed to see the other person relax? Because this afternoon could have been one of my nicest afternoons on record.

"Those boys are too dreamy. I have told you this before, many times." Desi chimes in.

"I know! But before these last couple of days he was so intense and weird and, let's face it, so was I." I groan and flop backward in my chair.

"He's so nice Desi. I want to… I want…" I sigh.

"You want to get greasy and naked with him. I know, Honeycake."

"I have a feeling you won't tell me, but do you know how this ends?" I ask her, squinting one eye at her from my flopped position on my chair.

Desi's magic isn't like looking into a crystal ball. She can't just look at someone and know what's going to happen. I think that choices play a role in her gift. She sees the possibilities once someone makes a choice… but not for everyone and not all the time. Magic is slippery like that. But if she has an inkling that this will crash and burn all around me, I want a heads up. Even if she can't tell me outright. She stops swirling the spoon around her mug of dandelion tea and looks over at me.

"I don't babe. I get good vibes from him though, from Tate too. Those two are some of the good ones. I want to shake their mama's hand if I ever meet her."

Desi shuffles over to me in her big slippers and settles herself into the love seat next to me. It's velvet and green and has been in her home as far back as I can remember. I have always sat in this loveseat with her, and I hope that I always will. Handing me the mug of tea, she tucks a loose strand of my ever-moving hair behind my ear.

"I don't think we will, Des, they live with Aunt Jett. I don't think their folks have been in town at all since they moved here last year." I wasn't entirely sure, but I got the feeling that Seb's parents aren't around anymore. He was gruff and cagey when the topic of family had come up earlier today, he seemed uncomfortable talking about them and only briefly mentioned his grandparents before swiftly shifting the conversation towards my family.

Which I quickly deflected as my mother then barged in like an embarrassing tornado, because *Alma*. I love her so much, but Jesus on a unicorn, my mom is a lot. Her visit was brief and intense, as usual. Which honestly I was grateful for since Seb and I were finally communicating meaningfully, I didn't want to derail all of our hard work by throwing my mother into the mix.

"I know, but if I ever meet her I intend to hug her and thank her for those men." she shivers comically, her expression lascivious. "I want to rub my face all over that scruffy hunk."

I laugh at her expression, as she continues to waggle her eyebrows suggestively. I'm aware that she and Tate have been flirting openly with each other for months now.

For as long as Seb and I have been warily circling each

other like badgers, Tate and Desi have been winking and flirting and generally being adorable. I try to squash down the surge of envy I feel. Desi has always been the braver witch, has always been confident and easy around others. I often wish I could bottle up some of her sureness and fill in some of my wary edges with her bravery.

"Are we still on to forage at McLaren's Wood tomorrow night?" I ask her, shifting the conversation away from my anxious feelings.

The moon will be full and there are a handful of plants I want that are best picked under a full moon. Plus the weather is supposed to turn after next week and I don't want to have to trudge out to the woods in the rain if I don't have to.

"You bet we are. I've got something I want to get my hands on up there myself"

Chapter 18

Seb

"Hey man, are you listening?" Tate calls to me from the other side of the workroom.

"Huh?" I respond distractedly. I'm definitely not listening. At all.

I'm picturing Cora yesterday in the shop.

We had spent the whole day together working on something she called "merchandising", which looks a lot like moving things around and stepping back to stare at it. Then moving something else and then adding a plant.

It is still baffling to me, but she was humming with happiness while we did it, and that had made my Wolf happy, so I'm not complaining. After our charged moments before lunch, we had spent the rest of the day comfortably together. Neither of us able or willing to break the spell between us.

We had talked about a lot of nothing, but in the spaces between the words we spoke, we told each other a lot more about ourselves than we ever had before. I now know that she has a sharp eye and a sharper tongue. She is funny and sarcastic and has an almost encyclopedic memory for herbs. She fiercely loves her shop and Desi and her intensely outlandish and eccentric mother who had walked in at one point to pick something up from the back room.

After bursting through the front door like a stylish and self-possessed Cosmo Kramer, Alma had swirled into the shop and taken me in with her shrewd gaze in a heartbeat. She kissed Cora's cheek before stalking over to where I was standing near the check-out desk and asked me to reach something from a shelf above us. When I brought it down, she grabbed my shirt in her fists and pulled me in close to her face in a surprisingly strong grip, and warned me, hissing low,

"If I find out that you have broken her heart at any time, there will be no body to find, Darling."

I blinked at her, nodded and mumbled a respectful "Ma'am" at her. She is a tiny woman and positively terrifying, even my Wolf recognized her authority and curled up inside me, getting as much space as he could. After searching my eyes for what felt like an uncomfortably long time, she seemed satisfied and nodded her head once.

Then she smoothed out my shirt and swirled away from me.

"Cora, My Treasure, have you run your hands over that brute's chest? His brawn is positively scrumptious!" She trilled as she swept towards the front door.

"MOM!" Cora had shrieked.

Cora's cheeks were beet red and she quickly covered her face in her hands, muttering something under her breath that sounded suspiciously like "Jesus h fuck."

I chuckled and watched her as she dragged her hands down her face while rolling her eyes back in her head dramatically.

"Language, Cora dear!" Her mother practically sang over her shoulder as she flourished a scarf over her shoulder and left the shop as quickly as she had arrived.

"Uuuuugh for fuck's sakes." Cora sighed once the door had clicked behind her mother.

"She seems… nice?" I said and Cora huffed a strangled laugh.

"She is nice. Also so, so embarrassing. Imagine her at middle school PAC meetings." She snarked as she rolled her eyes again. I smiled at the image, thankful that the conversation about my own family was cut short. I wasn't ready to admit to her yet that I had no knowledge of where my parents are. I didn't want to see the pity in her eyes.

We had spent a little more time talking about her mom's antics and some time discussing the remaining display design and generally had a good day together.

I shake off the memories and look over at my brother.

"What are you talking about, I wasn't listening." I said.

"Oh I know you weren't. You were mooning over Cora. I can tell. You have a face."

"What does that mean, "I have a face", we all have a face." I question, glaring at him.

"Nah dude, you have a Cora Face. You only make it when you are thinking about her. It's moony as fuck." He chuckles as he comes further over to my side of the room.

"I don't have a "moony" face, dude." I grumble.

He just shrugs his shoulders, still grinning at me.

"What were you talking about then?" I snarl.

"We need to run tonight. You haven't shifted in a few days and the moon is full. You are going to get rangy if you leave it any longer. I caught you growling at the chickens this morning."

I frown. I hadn't realized the full moon was tonight.

I've been so caught up in building this furniture for Cora and Desi that I've lost track of the time.

"I wasn't growling at the chickens." I grumble. "My stomach was rumbling because they look tasty and Aunt Jett has been feeding them so much. I want to eat them."

Tate barks out a laugh at me and claps my shoulder.

"Sure dude, whatever. In any case, I am going to run through McLaren's tonight, and you need to come too." He bounces on his feet a few times and shakes his shoulders.

"I also need to shift and it's a clear night."

"Yeah, I do too," I mutter. As much as I bristle at my brother, I know he is right. My Wolf agrees and growls in my chest. Tate gives me a cocked eyebrow at the sound and I roll my eyes back at him.

"I want to get this joint set and the legs sanded, and then we can head out after dinner."

Tate grins at me again and saunters back towards the front of the workshop.

The air tonight is clean and crisp and smells like there might be snow soon. I wonder briefly what winter in Eliza Falls will be like. This will be our first full turn of the seasons here, and based on the summer celebrations that popped up all over town, I expect the locals to go all out. I shudder as I recall Aunt Jett and her gaggle of elderly friends at the summer bonfire. That is an image I don't want to hold on to.

Before leaving the workshop tonight, Tate and I had tied up the last few details on the display for Cora and Desi and then walked home to Aunt Jett's to help her with dinner. The display is one of the best pieces I've built to date. It's elegant and solid, and I feel anticipation thrum through me when I imagine Cora's response to the finished piece. I really want her to love it.

The chickens are pecking around on the back porch as we get in, the matriarch getting persnickety when Tate tries to catch her.

"Why can't you just leave them alone? It's weird enough that they already think they run the place." I ask him.

"I don't know what it is about The Dame, but I want to snuggle her so bad." He laughs back at me as we watch the hen in question. She glares her beady eyes at him and scratches at the porch door.

Aunt Jett swings the door open, looks around wildly, and tumbles out.

"Oh, boys! Good, you're here already!" She huffs at us. Her apron is on askew and the usual snug bun at the back of her head is in disarray.

Tate and I share a look and take the last few steps up the back porch. Jett is breathing heavily, and her eyes dart around at all of the chickens on the porch.

"I need one of you to run over to the man cave and grab me the big copper pot that's in the bathroom."

"Aunt Jett," Tate starts, he furrows his brow at me and then looks back to Jett, "Why is there a big copper pot in the bathroom?"

"I needed *somewhere* to put the turtle and The Captain was getting surly with the poor dear. Your bathroom seemed like the best place to let him rest."

"The Captain is in our bathroom?"

"No Lovie, the turtle, keep up."

My eyes widen and I look closer at Aunt Jett. Upon closer inspection, she does look like she had to wrangle the angry rooster and paid the price for it.

"Why is there a turtle in our bathroom?" I ask her slowly.

"Well, I couldn't very well leave him in the kitchen!

Turtles are harbingers of disease, Sweetheart, and I am trying to get a roast in the oven." She says primly. Dusting her hands off like that is the most logical explanation and we are moving on, she turns on her heel and walks back inside.

Tate laughs and turns to go to our apartment, I follow Jett slowly into the main house.

Tate returns shortly afterward with the pot from our apartment, having placed our new roommate into the bathtub instead. When he brings it down to Jett, she kisses him on the cheek and tells him to put it out into the backyard. Shooting him a bewildered glance, I shake my head and shrug. I don't follow Jett's logic, and I'm not interested in dealing with a surprise turtle or a pissed off chicken, so I let it go.

Once we get dinner cleaned up and the dishes done, Aunt Jett wishes us both a "good run" and sends us on our way. The drive out to McLaren's Wood is peaceful tonight. The weather is holding out, the pressure of a change singing on the wind. The darkening sky reveals the glitter of stars and the foliage is holding on for a little while longer, gold and copper leaves looking deeper in the twilight. I breathe the evening air deep into my lungs, letting it settle into me and fill me up. The route to get to the park isn't long and we don't pass anyone else on the road. Now that the temperature drops more drastically when the sun sets, most people tuck themselves inside. We will have the park to ourselves, and my Wolf stretches in pleasure at the thought of an uninterrupted run.

"She's getting odder lately." Tate remarks as we pull the truck into the lot at the end of the drive. The provincial park is a protected area with a lot of unused trails that have been fenced off for years. It is the perfect place to go for a run and shift when we need to. When we come out here to run at night, we don't often see many other people on the trails. And we venture far enough into the woods before shifting so that we don't need to worry about a late season hiker sending in a Wolf sighting to the ranger's office, just in case.

There are natural wolves to the north of the area as well, so we feel safe in our Wolf forms whenever we run out here, as humans are pretty good at justifying what they want to believe. It's easier for them to assume we are outliers from the northern pack than to jump to the conclusion that we are actually werewolves.

"I think she spends too much time by herself." I reply. Jett is a cool old lady and I have already considered some ideas to get her around more people. She's got a little coven of old biddies who get together every once and a while, but I think she could use a little more regular socializing. The incident with the turtle tonight solidifies my suspicions. Although knowing Jett, she might just make the rest of her gaggle more eccentric, rather than the other way around.

We hike along one of the trails that veers deeper into the woods before being fenced off in a dead-end, the shorter path to the South connected into a loop as a redirection for casual hikers.

Tate and I hop the fence and keep walking along the old trail, deeper into the trees. After about a kilometre, the trail thins out into a series of meadows, which is where we plan to shift.

Chapter 19

Cora

"Oooh, the air feels flirty tonight!" Desi exclaims.

We parked my little hybrid in the South lot of McLaren's Wood Provincial Park and have bundled ourselves up for our late-night adventure. I have a backpack prepped with linen bags to collect my treasures, and Desi has a little woven basket to match her red hooded coat.

"I like that you kept your accessories thematic tonight, D." I say to her, smiling.

She twirls and laughs in response. "I couldn't resist when I remembered that I have this jacket."

"Did you pack any snacks in there?" I ask her, realizing that she likely did. We have a long history of late-night adventuring together and there are always snacks.

"Who do you take me for? An amateur? I know my grumbly Princess Peach needs her protein."

Laughing, I nudge her shoulder as we walk side by side over to the trailhead.

These trails are often busy during the summer and sometimes through the autumn during the day. But once the chill air settles in around mid-September, most locals steer clear after dark.

I'm looking forward to reaching the little series of clearings that I often visit for harvesting. It's a seasonal ritual for me to gather what I can find for my tea blends and salves as locally as possible, and I love this particular spot.

The moon is full tonight and the night is pretty clear, but the trees around the trail are dense and thickly packed together, so I pull my headlamp out from my bag and get it settled over my ponytail. On a brighter evening I would have suggested that we leave them, but tonight they are necessary. The last thing I need is to twist an ankle and hobble around for the next week. Or trip and fall into a gully which I may or may not have done on this foraging trip in years past. That was the last year we didn't pack the headlamps and I felt like we were evolving into our grown-up lady pants. Lessons learned and all that.

We adjust our respective bags and baskets, and start to hike along the paths silently, enjoying the quiet sounds of the forest at night. An owl hoots nearby, the underbrush rustles with the footsteps of someone small and furry, and far in the distance I think I hear a soft howl.

"Your outfit might be more appropriate than we thought tonight," I say softly to Desi, "I wonder if that was the big bad wolf we just heard."

She grins at me, waggling her eyebrows.

"I hope he's ready for me."

We laugh and continue along the trail. We've made this familiar trek so often together, I barely have to pay attention to where I am placing my feet anymore. This forest has seen me through a lot of my formative years, and I hope that I am still traipsing through these trees when I am old and wrinkly. There is a senior troupe from the local coven that practices rituals out here in the summer. An open invitation to other locals and even some favourite repeat visitors is put out every time they send out a newsletter and it's become one of the town's annual attractions. Humans and some non-local witches from nearby communities make the trip to enjoy a weekend of surfing, hiking and the occasional nude bonfire. Other towns claim their fame with a giant roll of string, so this isn't so offbeat. The gatherings move indoors to the community center once the weather shifts in the autumn, ever since some of the more outspoken members demand nudity for some of the more structured holiday rituals. No one is surprised to know that Jett is one of the loudest voices in *that* camp. Where some towns have Scout and Guide troupes, Eliza Falls has coven branches. The littlest witchlings are as young as four, and it's disgustingly cute.

Soon Desi and I reach the smaller, unmarked path that leads to the first clearing and where I want to stop first. There is a little patch of lavender that will likely be lush and ready for harvesting.

We clamber through the sparse section of bushes that hides the smaller trail from the main walking path and pick our way towards our first destination. Desi hums and reaches out to touch the mossy branches that hang over the trail, occasionally pointing out a particular collection of lichen or other interesting treasure she sees. I envy her easy way of walking through the world. I spend too much time hiding, keeping my head down, avoiding connections just in case I slip up in my control and then might break my heart.

I don't love that my first reaction to things is often to shy away from it or immediately squash my magic so I don't flare in front of anyone. I imagine it feels pretty amazing just letting the proverbial freak flag fly, flipping a middle finger or two to anyone or anything that tries to push you into a safe container. I've been jamming myself into my own safe container since I was seven years old and I kind of hate it. Actually, I really fucking hate it.

Maybe this thing between Seb and I could be so much more than this tense, flirtatious dance we've been doing. I think I am ready to have my feet stepped on a little and let him lead. The pull I feel towards him is so much more than anything I have felt for a partner before. I've been in relationships in the past, but nothing that I let get too serious.

Knowing that I am the reason my dad left us tends to clam up the old vulnerability and openness can of worms, and I would leave before anything got too serious. Before I had to introduce them to my mom or explain that they can't sleep over because I might accidentally set the sheets on fire if we got too passionate. The looks I got from one boyfriend after he counted the number of fire extinguishers in my apartment was enough to shut that one down. Big feelings always make my magic flares worse, so my modus operandi in all of my previous relationships was to keep it casual. Once I started to notice either of us catching feelings, I bolted.

But Seb feels so different. As much as I tried to keep my distance from him for the past year, I kept finding myself running into him. I'm not too embarrassed to admit that I might have Veronica Mars'ed his routine so I could "accidentally" bump into him a time or two. I resisted accepting that he was into me for so long, because if he was actually interested in me, and not just a grumpy, awkward asshole, then I would have to run him off. And even though it's what I have always done before, I didn't want to push him away after a while. Oh, I have definitely been a snarky, certified honey badger around him and also directly to his face over the last year. That's clearly on record. But the walls around me are crumbling fast under his tender assault now. Spending these last few weeks together, actually talking to each other, has battered my defenses into a soggy piece of bread. I want him to win.

Oh shit.

I want him to win. Gods dammit all, I am falling in love with him. My heart rate speeds up as I have my internal epiphany and I try desperately to get my shit together. I can be reasonable. Sure I kind of, sort of, never have before. In the field of love I am generally a sideline, waterboy type player. But I can be a cool quarterback, power forwardy, shooter type player. I'm sure those are sports words for important team people. The ones who score. I can do that.

Abruptly, Desi slows her steps, her head tilted to the left like she hears something. I wouldn't have noticed it if I hadn't been walking behind her and happened to be looking in her direction when she reacted. But I stop, waiting for her vision to pass. She does this sometimes, little flashes of something will creep up on her. More often than not it looks like a sneeze or like she's lost in thought. She gives a little shake like she is clearing her head or shivering from a sudden breeze. When she turns around to look at me, her expression is open and a little too bland while she blinks slowly in the light of my headlamp for a moment.

"I'm glad we decided to come out here tonight." Is all she says to me, softly and slowly, before turning around and walking on.

Ooookay.

Chapter 20

Seb

Tate has already shifted and is shaking himself out nearby. His Wolf is a big, shaggy, golden monster of a creature that could pass for a family dog if you squinted at him the right way. A very, very large, slightly terrifying dog.

Much like his human form, Tate as his Wolf is friendly and gregarious. He bounds around and generally enjoys himself. It's not something that we have ever done before, but we have joked that his Wolf could walk next to me in town and we'd probably get away with it.

I am slower to shift tonight. My thoughts keep straying to Cora and the last few days we've shared. It feels like we have reached a tipping point between us. There is so much tension, on both sides. I can't stop *gazing* at her. That's the only way to describe my moonstruck staring. Everything about her is luring me closer like she's a flamingo-haired siren calling my Wolf to smash himself on her shoreline.

Jesus Christ, now I am even thinking about her in poetry.

The pull of the Mate Bond isn't the only thing drawing me towards her anymore. The last few weeks I have been lucky enough to spend with her have only solidified my attraction. She's brilliant, funny and she loves people so hard. I've watched her interact with half of the town since Tate and I started this project with them, and she is the salty glue that holds so many pieces of this weird fucking town together.

She really listens to people when they talk to her and she holds space for people in a way that makes them feel like they are a treasured family member. Old Jim's grand-kids had come in one morning, shoulders hunched and metaphorical tails between their legs. It was just Cora and I working in the shop, and I watched her get right down to their level. The little one, Phoebe, was scowling, fury and embarrassment rolling off of her in waves. Her brother was a stoic wall of support behind her, while Cora slowly pulled the story out of them. Phoebe had bitten someone in her class, and had been suspended from school, the kids afraid to tell their mother. They came to Cora instead.

Cora shifted her body so that she could sit on the floor and pulled the little girl into her lap. She brushed her tangled hair away from her face, and cupped Phoebe's cheek, letting the little girl's tears fall into her hands. She was so soft and patient with them and was able to get to the bottom of WHY Phoebe had bitten the other child. Cora listened to what this other kid had done to deserve it; tormenting a bird that had flown into a school window and broken a wing, how Phoebe had fought the bigger kid to make them stop, earning herself a black eye and torn dress. Phoebe's brother Jace was beaming with pride for his sister, and Cora had smiled so brightly and hugged the little girl so tightly that she had squeaked. With their heads all bent together I couldn't entirely make out what she whispered to them while I was pretending to be busy on the other side of the store, but the kids left shortly afterwards with their heads held high and light steps.

She heard them and supported them and treated them as fully capable people. I want her to love me like that.

My Wolf purrs in my chest whenever we think about her, and tonight I sound like an engine idling. Shaking myself to clear my thoughts, I look up into the night sky. There is no cloud cover tonight and the bright, full moon gives us plenty of light to see by.

My Wolf is ready to run, and I feel the surge of adrenaline pumping through me. I love nights like this. Being out in the clean air and having just my brother here with me to share the experience. Our Wolves have been running together ever since our first shift when we were just pups, and we are both happier when we get to do this regularly.

Out of the corner of my eye I see Tate shoot off like a rocket after something and I roll my eyes. There is no tension coming from Tate through the pack bonds, just excited interest, so my Wolf isn't concerned by his sudden disappearance and I know that he isn't in any danger.

My Wolf's alpha nature feeds all of the pack bonds into me. As far back as I can remember, I have been the Alpha of our small pack. Even when I was a teenager being raised by our grandparents, my Wolf knew that we would lead one day. I can feel the connections we still have to Gamma and Gramps, a soft tether of light that ties us together as a family pack, even though they are hundreds of miles away. The bond tying me to Tate is bright and thick, a nearly tangible thread between us that lets me know that he's safe and well. I take some deep breaths while I soak in the moonlight and just sit in the feeling of being here. My Wolf is pricking his ears, getting focused and ready to shift.

Tate comes bounding back into the small clearing with a wriggling creature in his jaws.

"If you aren't planning to eat that squirrel you need to let it go. We don't play with our food." I say to him, my voice rough around the edges as I get closer to my Wolf. I watch as Tate croons a little howl around the squirrel like he is telling me he wants to keep it.

I laugh at his antics and start to curl my shoulders forward, readying for my own shift. But I stop jerkily, making my Wolf growl in frustration.

The wind just shifted and an unexpected but achingly familiar scent drifts over me.

"Oh fuck." I groan.

Tate cocks his head to one side, still maintaining his hold on the poor creature in his mouth. He lifts his nose in the air, sniffing awkwardly around the terrified squirrel and his tail begins to wag, his bright green Wolf eyes looking at me.

"This is bad Tate, I already started shifting and I don't know if I can hold it back!" I grind out between my teeth. Sweat is beading on my skin and I'm clenching my fists hard as I turn my head to catch the sounds drifting towards us. Desi is humming something and I can hear Cora's soft breathing.

Fucking Hell, this is not how I want to tell her what I really am!

While I stand here like a deer caught in headlights, trying desperately to get my body moving, the two women walk right into the clearing. They are both wearing little lights on their heads like spelunkers, the beams sweeping across the forest floor as they pick their way through the underbrush. Cora stops abruptly when she sees that they aren't alone, but Desi walks right up to me.

"Hey Seb," she says casually. Like it was totally normal to run into me in the middle of the woods, in the dark.

"Desi." I growl.

"You're not alone in your feelings, Love." She whispers to me once she is close enough to speak quietly. My body jerks and I look sharply at Cora, who is cautiously stepping over to me.

"What are you doing out here? Are you ok? Why are you so sweaty??" She asks me. Her eyes are wide and her nostrils flare. Her sharp gaze flits between Tate's Wolf and me.

"Ughn?" is my cunning reply.

Tate bounds around in the little clearing behind me, the squirrel still held gingerly between his jaws. He flops to sit on the ground between us and looks adoringly at them. He's big enough in his Wolf form that he barely has to look up.

I still can't quite wrap my head around the fact they are here. My Wolf is pushing hard against the edges of my control. He wants her to see us as we really are, but this encounter is not how I expected to tell her, so I keep fighting him.

"Did you get a dog?" Cora asks slowly, head tilted, looking at Tate with a furrowed brow.

Tate drops the squirrel, licking his muzzle, the little rodent lays on the ground heaving, looking the worse for wear after being drooled all over by my ridiculous brother.

"Uh, not exactly." I'm hedging and twitching with the need to complete my shift soon, but I need her to be ready. I need her to be ok.

"How do you not exactly get a dog? Is he one of your brother's fosters? Is Tate out here too?" She looks at him again and her head quirks over to the other side, really looking at him with narrowed eyes.

"What kind of dog even is this? He's weirdly big. Like, scary big."

The squirrel stumbles away and I grab Tate by the scruff to keep him from chasing after it again. This is getting absurd. Tate thumps his tail and his tongue lolls out the side of his mouth. He scoots a little closer to Desi and she croons at him.

"Oh Cora, my obtusely adorable Crabcake, it's Tate."

"Tate??" Cora exclaims, her eyes widening at me now.

I shift uncomfortably, looking over at Desi with wonder. How does she know?

How could she possibly know that? My mind is spinning, running over every encounter we've had with these women. There has always been something about Desi that had piqued my awareness, but my attention and my Wolf were always so focused on Cora that I had clearly repressed that curiosity. Turning my attention back to Cora's stunned expression, I desperately search my mind for a plausible explanation, anything to defuse this insane situation. But my Wolf is pleased with this unexpected turn of events. Maybe this is the universe showing me the way forward. Perhaps hiding from Cora isn't what we need anymore. I clear my throat and take a chance. A chance that could change everything.

"Yeah, that's Tate."

She is watching me closely, really looking at me and I can't tell if she likes what she sees. It feels like an eternity while I stand in front of her, trying to will the Wolf back inside. But he is pushing towards Cora, like a compass yearns for the north star.

Inexorable and relentless. He needs her to understand.

"Seb," she says slowly, her voice awed, "are you guys… werewolves?"

I heave deep breaths and hold Cora's eyes, willing her to accept us. While I search for the right thing to say, Desi has gotten down on her knees in front of Tate and is petting his scruff and making cooing, baby noises at his Wolf. True to his nature, he is eating that shit up. He rolls over and gives her his belly.

"Jesus, Tate, get it together." I rasp at him. My ears are getting hot and my Wolf is getting harder to restrain. My whole body trembles with the effort to hold my Wolf back. I've tried desperately not to Wolf out in front of Cora. I try not to shift in front of *anyone*, but Cora is something else. I need her like nothing I've ever felt before. She's waiting for my response. The truth swirling between us like a typhoon.

My Wolf is still rumbling in my chest. Not a growl. It sounds like a purr, but deeper. He is trying to get closer to her, but I am trying really hard not to freak her the fuck out. But she doesn't look freaked out. Well, not too freaked out.

She is definitely looking at me warily, but that might have more to do with my stammering and idiotic responses to her questions and the fact that my werewolf brother is rolling around on his back now, chuffing at her friend. Who is now looking for a stick to throw for him.

"Come on you fluffy dreamboat! Let's go play while these two sort themselves out."

Desi smiles at Cora, and makes a shooing motion towards her like she is ushering her closer to me. My Wolf starts rumbling louder in my chest as Cora returns her gaze to me. She scrunches her nose up, that expression that she makes when she is trying to puzzle something out, and crosses her arms over her chest. I can see her clever mind turning over this new information. She squints at me before she exhales sharply and straightens her shoulders. She clicks off her light, removes it entirely and pulls her pack from her shoulders and drops it on the ground before rubbing her hands together.

"Alright Seb, let's do this."

She heaves out another breath like she is letting go of something heavy, pulls the tie from her hair, and closes her eyes. My eyes adjust to the sudden lack of light quickly and I watch her, waiting to see what she is going to say next, marvelling at her unbound hair. I've never seen it down, and it's gorgeous. Wavy and long, the pink varies in shade from deeper at the root to lighter at the ends. But she doesn't look at me, and she doesn't say anything. Instead she lets her hands drop to her sides and takes another deep breath. The leaves around us start swirling in a gentle breeze that slowly picks up speed. But it's coming from her.

And it's warm. Her long hair floats around her head as if she is underwater, swirling languidly.

My Wolf watches intently, as intrigued as I am. What is she doing?

"Cora..."

She lifts her hands, palms facing upwards, blue flames dancing in her palms.

"Uh... Cora?"

"Shh, Seb, I am trying to open up here, this is hard for me and you are very distracting so please just shut up."

I shut up as instructed and just watch her as she mumbles something under her breath and then I stumble back as she levitates, just a little, off the ground. The warm, swirling wind moving around her picks up speed, and it starts whipping her hair around her. She is like a living candle or a crackling fire, all heat and swirling embers.

My Wolf is wildly in love with her already, this display

of her magic only solidifying his awe, and I can feel him pushing against my skin. We were already so close to shifting when the women had stumbled onto us that it's taking a lot of my energy to keep it under control. But what Cora is currently doing is like nothing I've ever seen before.

She settles herself back on the ground again, the wind slows down and the flames in her palms shrink and extinguish themselves, pulling back into her body. She takes another deep breath and opens her eyes. Looking right at me she says, "I'm an earth witch."

Huffing out my own deep breath I take a step towards her. She doesn't step back. She has taken a leap of faith. By exposing herself to me in this way, she has created a safe space for me to do the same. She's made space for *me*. Showing me her magic has filled her with a quiet confidence that she usually keeps hidden. She isn't avoiding my eyes, she's holding them. I love it.

So does my Wolf.

"Cora…" I start. But instead of more words, words that I don't always have to fill in the gaps of my feelings, I honour her bravery with some of my own. I show her.

I close my eyes and let my Wolf flow over me. The air shimmers around my body and soft, dark fur ripples around me as I curl down towards the ground to stand on four legs. My change is smooth and fast, my Wolf eager to display his form to her. I shake myself out and stand still before her.

Cora gazes at me with wide eyes and she reaches her hand out. She catches herself, like she didn't mean to put her hand out towards me. But I chuff at her and she blinks. While she holds herself still, I slowly pad closer to her. I rub my muzzle against her hand and she lets out a soft breath, like a gasp.

"Holy shit Seb, this is so fucking wild." She rasps quietly under her breath. Like she doesn't want to startle me, but can't keep the words in.

She keeps her hand out and I shamelessly rub against it, pushing my body closer to her. She curls her fingers into my ruff and it feels so good. In all the time we have spent together lately, this is the first time that she has touched me on purpose. We have shared a few accidental touches. I ran my hands down her arms one afternoon when I could no longer resist touching her, but she's never put her hands *on me* before this. I can feel her touch through my fur and deep into my bones. I grumble low in my chest, overjoyed that she is touching me. Pleased that we aren't hiding from each other anymore.

Chapter 21

Cora

He is *so big*.

I mean, he was big before when he was standing in front of me looking embarrassed and a little panicky. Tate and Desi are off in the next little clearing and Seb and I just… stand at each other. Just for a moment before I decide to trust myself. Trust this feeling I have about him and open up.

I've shown him my magic and he didn't run away screaming. And he has shifted into a Wolf.

Like, an actual enormous, hulking wolf. Because. He. Is. A. Werewolf.

So unbelievably cool.

His silky snout is high enough to nuzzle my armpit and he is comfortably nosing me all over, sending little thrills of goosebumps all over me where he touches me. The back of my neck feels tingly and my hands are a little bit shaky as I push my hands over his shoulders, delving into the thick fur there. His fur is so soft! Much softer than I expected a wolf's fur to be. But in my limited exposure to Wolves (read zero) I don't have much to go on, so I don't know why I am surprised. Also, *magic*.

I lean my body into him and push my face into his rumbling chest. He snorts a little breath, like he is surprised maybe? Like he doesn't expect me to accept him. Like maybe people don't let him in and he expects me to run. My heart cracks open for him a little more at that thought, because I do that. I push people away, thinking that I am protecting myself. But I've been hurting them too. Gods dammit, self-realization sucks balls.

My heart speeds up when he tucks his big, wet nose into my hair and softly breathes me in. His breath is hot against my skin, and it makes liquid heat pool deep in my belly. He runs his soft muzzle along my neck and behind my ear, his whiskers tickling and making me shiver in response. Electricity zings up my spine and I lean into him more, pushing my face into the soft ruff of fur at his shoulder.

"I see you, Seb." I whisper, and I wrap my arms around his big neck.

He stills. His body feels hot and hard under all that fur and then he shudders. His whole form ripples under my hands until he is kneeling in front of me. My arms are still wrapped around his neck and while there is a part of my brain that really wants to know how that works, how I was one moment hugging a giant wolf, and now I am leaning into Seb's big, muscled chest. The bigger part of me, the part that I have been pushing down, down so deep and far away, opens up and I hug him harder.

His big arms wrap around my smaller body tentatively and he gently holds me. Like I am a bird he's caught in his hands, like I am something precious. I can feel his heartbeat pounding against my cheek when I press my face into his chest.

"It's ok." I say quietly. "I won't freak out."

He hugs me harder then, like it's too much. Like it's what he's been hoping for.

I can still hear his Wolf rumbling in his chest, and I realize that I like it.

I pull back a little bit, just enough so that I can look into his face. His expression is open, hesitant. But I can feel his heart in his gaze as we look at each other. He doesn't move as I shift my body so that I can stand up in front of him. He is so much taller than me that he stays on his knees while I stand, looking up at me. I press my hands onto his shoulders and he keeps his arms wrapped loosely around me while I move. His breathing is coming in fast, quiet pants, which tell me he is fighting something still.

But he lets me lead this moment.

I move my hands to his face, tracing my fingers along his jaw, cupping his cheeks and pushing his hair off his forehead with hands that tremble a little. His arms tighten slightly around me when I lean forward, his hands slide up my back and hold me against him. I keep my eyes locked on his the entire time, watching his reactions, seeing the flash of emotions dance through his eyes.

I brush my nose against his and he inhales deeply.

His eyes widen as I get close enough to softly brush my lips against his. His hands move gently up my spine and I nearly crumble when his thick fingers slide into my hair. The feel of his breath against my lips is like nothing I have ever felt before, tender and desperate in equal measure. His breath fans across my face as I close my eyes and let myself feel everything about this moment.

I kiss him. Softly, so softly, so I don't break whatever spell is dancing around us. I press my mouth against his, tasting him, feeling how hot his skin is. He's like a sultry wood stove on a winter night, all encompassing, sinking into my bones to warm me from the inside out.

He breathes me in and I open my lips slightly, running the tip of my tongue across the seam of his mouth.

He twitches against me, groans into my mouth, deep and rumbly, and then *he* is kissing *me*. He slants his head over mine and turns this moonlit magic moment into something visceral and heavy. Our tongues slip and slide against each other in a ritual as old as the stars.

When he bites my lower lip, my eyes nearly roll back into my head.

He kisses me so deeply and holds me so tightly that I moan into his mouth as we push our bodies closer together. I want to be closer to him, a part of him. Somehow all of the yearning and want of the last year cascades into me all at once and I need him to devour me.

He holds me so tight that when I gasp at the feel of his hips rolling into mine, he swallows the sound in another fierce kiss that evolves from the last, all of them robbing me of any coherent thoughts.

His hands move over my body roughly. Like he wants to squeeze our bodies even closer together and I moan again, pushing my breasts into his chest. His Wolf is constantly growling from inside him, the sexiest purr that makes his whole body vibrate.

Our hands are everywhere, mine in his hair, his on my ass, we can't stop touching each other, kissing each other like we will literally die if we stop, and I never want to stop. Why have we not been doing this the whole time?? This feels so good, so intensely right. Like our souls have just been waiting for our stubborn brains to get caught the hell up already and we consume each other like we're starving. It's *amazing*.

"Cora," he groans against my lips. "My Cora."

I don't know if he means to say that out loud, but hearing it sends a torrent of delight all over my body, and my fingertips start tingling. Instead of the icy grip of panic, all I feel is glad.

I realize that I want to be his.

I can feel his cock pushing against my belly, hard and urgent. We are pressed so close to each other that there is no way I could miss it and I grind myself against him. I rub against that thick length, chasing my greedy pleasure. He growls low, the vibrations surging through his body, straight to my clit, and then somehow, like dirty sex magic, we are on the ground and he is All. Over. Me. He is kissing me and stroking his big hands all over my body and I shamelessly writhe under him.

He pushes his hips into mine and I gasp again as I feel his stiff cock push against my pussy through our clothes. Why are we wearing so many damned clothes?!

"Oh Gods, Seb! *Yes.*" I sigh into his mouth.

He grinds his hips harder into me and I love it. I wrap my legs around his hips and squeeze him tighter against me while our mouths tangle together and we are both heaving and moaning on the forest floor. In the back of my mind, I know that Tate and Desi have left the clearing. They are giving us space to explore this thing between us. Desi would have known what we were going to do before we did and she took Tate with her.

I know we are alone.

I inhale again when Seb starts kissing along my jaw. I arch underneath him, showing him my throat and he shudders over me. He draws a ragged breath in as he runs his nose along my exposed neck, taking in my scent. His teeth drag along my skin, just under my ear and it's my turn to shudder.

"Cora, wait, are you sure?" He whispers raggedly into my ear.

"Yes Seb, oh Gods yes." I take a deep breath in, realizing that I trust him and my feelings for him are bigger than I ever thought possible. I realize at that moment that I need us to come together.

"If we do this, if we keep going, I won't be able to stop. My Wolf…" He pauses, gulping deep breaths of air into his lungs, fisting his hands into my wild hair. Maybe he's trying to settle some of the wild energy around us, between us? All I know is that it's hot as hell.

"My Wolf wants to claim you so badly Cora, and once we do, he won't let you go. I need you to understand what that means."

His breathing is strained, ragged, while he looks deep into my eyes.

I know this. I know that once we take this step together, there is no going back. But going back is no longer an option.

Chapter 22

Seb

Cora's body is heaving underneath me, she's rolling her hips up against my cock, unravelling my jagged control and I strain to wait for her. I need her to accept us, I won't push her into this. She needs to understand that the choice is hers and that her choice will change everything between us forever.

"No going back?" She whispers.

"You are my Mate, Cora, I can't go back. But I won't push you. I will wait forever for you."

"Oh Seb," She sobs.

She reaches up and pulls my mouth down to hers again and kisses me hard. Our teeth clash together with the frenzy of desperation surging through us and she moans into me, rocking her core against my achingly hard dick. Jesus Christ, the feeling of her underneath me like this is nearly too much to handle. My Wolf is howling, telling me to claim her, bite deep into the tender flesh of her neck. He wants me to take her fully, to push inside and pump her full of us. I snarl as I roll us over so that she is riding me. I need her to have more control. Her legs spread wide over my hips and she grinds down against my cock. She finds a rhythm and uses me to chase her pleasure.

She sits up, breathing hard, looking deep into my eyes.

My Wolf stills, watching her.

"I want this Seb. I want us. I can't stop thinking about you."

My Wolf howls inside me, pleased with our Mate. Her acceptance flows over me like the shift and I groan out loud and sit up to kiss her again. I need there to be no distance between us, so I hold her against me, one hand wrapped around her back like a vice as she presses herself tightly to me. We are frantic then, both of us pulling at each other's clothes, desperate to feel skin.

"Get this shirt off, Seb!" she cries, yanking on the buttons of my flannel shirt.

I wrangle my arms out of it as quickly as I can, while I pull at her belt.

"I am going to fuck you so hard." she growls at me. Cora, my quiet, reserved and wary Mate is growling *at me.* I nearly go cross-eyed with delirious joy. She pulls my shirt off and kisses me again, her mouth suddenly everywhere. She kisses my face, my ears, she rubs her cheeks across mine, and I love it. She is marking me, and my Wolf is practically howling with pleasure.

I fumble at her waist to pull her pants down her hips and she rolls over onto her side.

"Pullthemoffpullthemoff!" She hisses, pushing her tight jeans down her legs and I yank them off her feet.

"Oh my Gods, Cora, you are so hot." I grunt while I shove my own pants down my legs. I stare at her, standing above her like this, and drink in the sight of her. Her skin is smooth over lean muscles and her trim waist flows beautifully to slim hips. I let my gaze travel over her small breasts, peaked with hard pink tips, her chest flushed just like her cheeks. My cock twitches, bouncing in the night air as her eyes make their way across my body too.

Reaching for me again, Cora pulls my big body over hers and we grasp at each other, our hot flesh rubbing together, making me fucking crazed. Our bodies are completely naked now and I have no idea where our shirts went or when they came off.

She spreads her legs wide underneath me and I can feel the heat of her cunt against my aching cock and I groan desperately into her mouth.

"Fuck, Cora, you feel so good. Your scent is driving me mad."

"Keep talking, oh Gods, I love dirty talk!" She whines back at me.

"Tell me what you want Cora, tell me how you want me to fuck you."

Whimpering now, she arches her back underneath me and reaches for my hand.

"Touch me, Seb, I want your hands on my tits."

Holy Shit.

I reach up and cover her soft breast with my hand. My rough fingers scrape against her nipple and she gasps. She reaches down between us and wraps her hot little hand around my cock and I nearly come on the spot.

"Ughhn! Cora!" I grit at her.

"SebSebSeb, yes, ohmygods you're so BIG, fuck, I can't wait to feel you inside me." The words tumble out of her mouth like she can't stop herself and I have to grit my teeth to hold back my release.

I pull her hand away from me and stretch it above her head.

"What, what are you doing, I thought…" She starts,

looking confused, cheeks flushed and eyes glazed, heaving deep breaths under me. The most beautiful sight I have ever seen.

"I am going to eat your sweet pussy." I rumble to her, staring into her wide eyes.

"Fuck yes." she breathes, and she reaches her free hand up to clasp my wrist that holds her other hand in a tight grip.

I trail my fingers softly over her ribs, down to her hips and follow it with my mouth over her skin, working my way down her body.

"Keep your hands above your head."

"Sure thing, will do." she giggles breathlessly.

Oh shit, her laugh is adorable.

I move my hands to her breasts, kneading them and rolling her nipples and she arches her back even more. Straining to have more of her, I latch my mouth on one perfect breast and suckle hard.

She cries out and covers her face with her hands.

"Put your hands back up." I order again. "Watch me fuck you with my mouth."

"Oh Gods!" she groans, her eyes rolling back up into her head as I lick and suck my way down to her slit.

I use my fingers to spread her pussy open for me and swirl my tongue around her clit. She shrieks and bucks against my face and I hold her still, my shoulder pressing her legs wide, hands on her trembling hips.

"This is mine." I growl at her.

"Fucking SHUT UP, Seb, and lick *my* cunt, you alpha son of a bitch." She hisses.

I chuckle at her sudden ferocity. Then follow instructions.

Chapter 23

Cora

Oh. My. Gods. *Ohmygods!*

Seb is *really* good with his mouth.

My whole body trembles with need and he is just getting started. He licks my pussy with long, sure strokes, his hot eyes on me the whole time. I am panting and can barely hold myself still while he strokes his tongue over my clit, over and over.

"I-I need more Seb." I pant.

He spreads my legs wider then, and moves his big body around so that he can place one of his huge hands against my inner thigh and his other hand up to trace my lower lips. I am pressed wide open underneath him, his weight the only thing keeping me from floating away.

"Oh shit, yes yes yessss." I moan.

He rubs his fingers into my wetness, rubbing little circles over my clit, and then slides one of his thick fingers inside me.

Oh fuck. I'm going to die here. This is it.

He's going to sex me to death, and I don't even care.

"Please, Seb, yes!" I think I am starting to speak in tongues. I don't even know what I'm saying anymore. He continues to hold my hips down and drags that big finger in and out of me. And then he leans back in, that delicious, beautiful son of a bitch, and sucks on my clit again. I scream.

I come so hard, twitching and crying out as my orgasm sweeps over me. A full-body, glorious orgasm takes me over, making me see stars. I'm barely coming back into myself as he chuckles into my cunt and curls his finger. He rubs against my G spot, and I come again, ohmygods I'm coming again!

Tears leak out of my eyes, and I am pulling his hair. I don't remember reaching down to grab his head, but I did and I am and I don't even care.

"Oh holy shit Seb." I pant, as my body melts into the ground.

"Fuck, Cora, you are delicious." He purrs at me, looking deep into my eyes as he sweeps his tongue over his lips and slowly crawls up my body.

"GGhnnhh." I reply. Completely at his mercy.

I try words again, "I-I, I think I need a minute big guy." I rasp out.

He kisses my tits and my shoulders and up my neck. His teeth graze along the tender skin behind my ear and my core floods with fresh desire.

"I am going to claim you, Cora." He whispers into my ear.

"I am going to slowly push my hard cock into your tight, wet cunt and I am going to Fuck. You. Now."

Dead. I am dead.

I nod my head at him because I can't speak now that I'm a sex ghost. I look him in the eye as he reaches down between us and wraps his big hand around his magnificent cock. Then I have to look. I watch him stroke that gorgeous length and line it up with my entrance.

He rubs the head of it in my juices, the contact hot and slick, and then slowly, so slowly! He pushes that monster inside me. I can feel the steady glide of him all through my already tenderized body.

"Oooohhhhh yessssss please!" I sob.

My hips are wiggling, trying to get him to get in me faster and he groans above me, the sound travelling through the head of his dick, and I think I might pass out.

"Fuck Cora, oh fuck, fuuuuck, you are so hot and tight." He groans as he pushes deep inside me and there is no more room, no more space between us. We stare at each other, chests heaving.

I run my hands over him, feeling all of his restrained power. He is breathing heavily, staring into my eyes. And then he starts to move. Slowly at first, he pumps that huge cock into me, over and over. Long, deep strokes that I feel *everywhere*. He is filling me up and I am already dead and I keep making breathy, gasping, moaning sounds.

He sinks his body lower over me and kisses me, moving his hips in a heady rhythm and consuming my soul so deeply and thoroughly that I am going to come again already. I wrap my legs around his waist, pulling him in deeper with each stroke and he growls low in his throat.

His pace speeds up, pushing us across the soft grass as he pumps faster and harder into me and I beg for more.

"Please Seb, oh gods yeah, just like that!" I keen into his mouth. I'm a wanton, thrashing creature of sex. He has unleashed something within me and now that she's out and has had his good stuff she is never going back in.

"Ohmygodsohmygodsohmygods." I'm muttering

gibberish and he is pumping faster now, and I'm crying out for more and he is sweating on me and I love it. Who *am I*?

"Cora I…we.." Seb grunts above me. I look into his eyes and I see his Wolf looking back at me.

"Me too, babe." I whisper.

He growls low again, and this time it vibrates his whole body. I can feel his cock, pumping in and out of me, start to vibrate too and my eyes widen.

"Yes, oh fuck yes Seb!" I cry out as another wave of intense orgasm sweeps me under and my muscles clench around him and then he is coming too.

He roars out above me, pushing his face into my neck, a searing flash of excruciating pleasure blasts through me as he shudders his release into me.

It takes us a few moments to calm our breathing down. Slowly coming back into my body after the most intense sexual experience of my life, I look up at him and grin.

"Death by Big Wolf Dick. Not a bad way to go."

Chapter 24

Seb

Cora and I lay panting together for what feels like hours.

I have finally claimed her and my Wolf is purring his smug satisfaction in my chest. It feels like my whole body is still vibrating and every once in a while Cora will shift and sigh. I'm still deep inside her. We are filling ourselves up with each other. I can't stop gazing at her and running my fingers through her soft, pink hair.

"You always wear your hair tied up because of your magic, don't you?" I ask her softly.

Her small smile tugs at my heart, and I want to rub my cheek against hers, inhale her scent.

Realizing that I can, I do exactly that. I close my eyes as I bend my head into the crook of her neck and shoulder, rubbing my nose and face into her hair. I lick over the bite I gave her, already smoothed over and looking like a spectacular hickey. She chuckles softly and squirms at my touch.

I feel my cock jerk inside of her and she gasps. Her eyes flood to black with heat and I growl deep in my throat.

"You always bolted when your Wolf got pushy didn't you?" She counters, her voice low and smokey. I continue to rub my nose into the side of her neck, and lick the shell of her ear.

"That's not fair!" She gasps again as I trail the tip of my tongue over her earlobe and then bite her gently. My cock thickens and she rocks her hips up into me, making me moan.

She is slick and hot and we start moving together again, our bodies rocking and our hands roaming. The intensity of our first mating had burned hot and fierce between us, but this time we kiss each other languorously, breathing into each other's mouths, gasping together.

My Wolf is finally content now that Cora is in our arms.

She runs her hands all over my shoulders and back, sending gooseflesh racing across my skin. I move over her, inside of her, my weight braced on my forearms, my hands in her hair. She takes all of me, meeting my movements with her own and our tempo increases. We stare into each other's eyes as we chase our pleasure. When she comes again, her body tensing under me and her sex clenching tight around my dick, I groan. My Wolf howls his satisfaction inside me as we come and I claim her again, my release marking her in hot jets of my seed.

Shuddering deep breaths, I watch Cora come down from her third or fourth orgasm of the night and soak up this moment with her. The moonlight spills across her flushed skin. We are both sweaty from our exertions, her skin pebbling in the night air now that our frenzy is receding.

"Are you cold?" I ask her. My bigger body is still wrapped around her, but I know that we can't stay here in the clearing all night.

She hums a response to me and inhales deeply before stretching her arms above her, her perfect breasts on display, her skin decorated with marks from my mouth.

"That was… something else Seb." She purrs. As if her body is still waking up, her movements are slow and sultry.

I chuckle at her expression, a mix of awe and want and wonder. I feel the same and I know that it will only get better between us, which seems impossible considering what we just did. It feels like she is the sun and I have no choice but to surrender to her gravity. I will do it happily and willingly for the rest of my life, circling around her orbit, chasing our stars.

"Can you walk?" I ask her, slowly making the moves to get up. I'm loath to pull out of her warmth, but if I don't I will work her up and take her again. Her stomach is growling and my Wolf wants to feed her and get her home. He wants to build her a nest and nourish her.

"Sex ghosts don't walk." She mumbles. "I'll just apparate home and haunt you until you have no choice but to use your evil sex magic on my spectre."

I chuff out a laugh and she groans as my hips pull away from her. I gaze at her body, the evidence of our activities shining between her legs and down our thighs and my Wolf growls his pleasure at the sight. I run my hands through it and up her hips and she gasps when I push my hands up her belly and over her breasts, massaging our mingled scents into her skin.

"Are all werewolves so pervy?" She hisses out at me as I roll a nipple and growl.

"Gods, Cora if you don't want me to fuck you again

right now you need to get dressed." I grit into her ear. She shudders and laughs, the sound full of heat.

"Get up then, Oh Wild One and throw me my shirt. This witch needs to eat." She smiles up at me, and kisses my nose.

My Wolf preens and recedes into me, feeling settled and pleased with our mate.

Chapter 25

Cora

Well. That was… mind-blowing? Life-altering? The most intensely satisfying, soul awakening sex-fest known to womankind?

Holy shit, Seb is bringing some serious heat and I'm still in a daze as we walk hand in hand back to his truck. We touch each other constantly, as if making up for lost time, neither one of us willing to pull away. We got dressed in awed silence, stealing glances at each other as we slowly added layer after layer. The heat in his eyes never dimmed and I feel a thrill dancing up my spine every time I think about what we just did. Great hairy balls of Zeus, what we just did! My core tightens as I look over at him again, I just can't stop mooning at him. And considering how many times he catches my eye when I do, he's in the same boat. I smile up at him as we get ourselves to the little parking lot, and his soft eyes sparkle in the moonlight.

I sigh as he slows to a stop and pulls his big hands up to cup my face and kiss me softly.

"Can I take you home, can I stay with you?" He asks me, his voice low and quiet. The warmth that has taken up residence in my chest stutters like a flame in the wind as a wave of uncertainty crawls up my throat, shutting down my good vibe endorphin party like a slamming door. I cram that mother fucker down deep into my subconscious.

This is ok, this is great in fact. This gorgeous, sexy, hot, hulking werewolf that I have been crushing on so hard and who just dicked me into oblivion wants to come to my house and snuggle me? Stop being stupid, Cora, say yes.

"Yes please." I breathe.

Once we are on the road and rumbling back to civilization, I pull my phone out of my backpack and read through the messages that Desi has left me.

Desi: Girlfriend you GET THAT

Desi: Tate is taking me back to their place for tonight, we don't want to get underfoot while you two bone down all night.

Desi: I will expect your report on my desk tomorrow young lady.

Desi: There is a protein bar in the outside pocket of your backpack, you need to fuel up.

Desi: I love you

I laugh quietly as I picture her skipping around the

woods with Tate in his big Wolf body, sneaking a snack into my backpack. I look over at Seb, his shirtsleeves are rolled up, forearms exposed as he keeps one hand gently on my knee and as he confidently steers the big truck with the other down the windy old road back towards town. I can't help but notice, yet again, that he has delicious forearms, powerful without being huge and dusted with soft hair. Am I drooling?? I shift my perusal over him as a whole and try not to perv on his arms like a thirsty teenager. His whole energy feels different now, settled, at peace even. His big shoulders are relaxed, the furrow between his eyebrows is gone, and I realize that I haven't really seen him look serene before, but it's definitely the vibe he is giving off right now. He has been holding himself so tight this whole time! A wave of compassion sweeps over me at the thought. If only I hadn't been so stubbornly defensive, I could have seen this softer side of him sooner. If only.

He glances over to me then and I feel my whole face light up. Sweet merciful Goddess, I am *beaming* at him. I don't think I have beamed at anything before in my life! His answering smile is so big and dreamy that I don't even care. I wink at him, die a little more inside when the big fucker *blushes*, and look back down to my phone to respond to Desi.

Cora: I love you too. Thank you for the bar, eating it now. Will write a report when I rise from the dead and can communicate in human language again.

I chuckle softly to myself as I put my phone away and break the bar in half. I pass one to Seb, and he smiles his sweet half-grin at me. The butterflies that have been catching their breath in my belly spring back to life and my whole body shivers with it.

I press my lips together to keep my smile to a reasonable level and nibble on my half of the bar as we drive home.

When we get to my apartment, we stay close to each other, constantly touching, like neither of us can stand to not be in contact. The tension between us is still classified as obscenely sexual, my body hyper-aware of the distance between his hot junk and my thirsty vagina. I send him sultry looks and his eyes, Gods help me, his eyes flood to black as midnight with his hunger. Giddy desire floods my synapses and I press myself against him.

His hard chest is constantly rumbling, and now that I know that he has a WOLF INSIDE OF HIM, it makes the sound that much more incredible. I run my hands over his chest, letting my fingers tease his beefy pectorals until I can't stand it anymore and I have to pull at his shirt again.

"Off, this needs to go." I demand, working my trembling fingers into the buttons and huffing in frustration when I can't get them undone fast enough. He hulk tears out of that shirt, buttons flying, and we are on fire, kissing frantically and tripping over every piece of furniture in my home. We stumble into the bathroom, trailing little bits of the forest floor after us, like breadcrumbs leading back to our glorious sex romp. We peel the layers of clothing off of each other with desperate reverence. Seb's eyes never leave my body as more and more of me is revealed.

I undo the buttons of his worn jeans and he runs his big hands over my hips. Soon we are both naked again, and the steam from the shower fills up the small room.

My bathroom feels even smaller with Seb's big body curling around mine as he pulls the elastic from my top knot and runs his fingers over my scalp and down through to the ends of my hair. His fingertips brushing over my bare shoulders sends shivers down to my toes.

"Get in the shower Cora, I want to wash you." He says. His voice is so deep it sounds like he is gritting his teeth against the rocks in his throat.

His big cock is pressed between us, precum dotting my belly and I turn around to step into the shower. He follows me in, closing the glass door behind him. The steam immediately envelopes us like a cloud and he runs his hands over my shoulders, down my back, and lightly scratches his nails over my ass.

I moan and push myself into him, feeling his erection twitch against my lower back.

He grunts and stills. Like he has to get control of himself, of his Wolf maybe, before he can move again. I love that I affect him like this. After nearly a year of pining over him and thinking about what it would be like to be naked with him, the reality far outshines my fantasy.

He heaves a deep, shuddering breath and grabs the soap from in front of me. He lathers up his hands and then runs his slick, impossibly hot hands over my skin. My skin pebbles and I hold as still as I can while he cleanses my entire body, methodically, reverently. He smooths his soapy hands across my belly, pulling our bodies closer together and I can feel his chest rumbling. His Wolf is purring deep and it shakes his whole body. My little pink vibrator is going straight into the trash tomorrow morning. How can my body be so needy for him again already? We just did this! I have become addicted to his touch in a very short time and right now I am not willing to get mad about it. I'm just going to enjoy this.

He runs his hands up to my breasts, and I lean my head back into his shoulder.

"Seb, please." I whimper. I push my backside into his

hips and his breath hitches in my ear. Growling low, he runs one slippery hand down to my aching cunt and slips two big fingers between my folds. I gasp and throw my hands against the wall of the shower, my knees starting to shake.

"Keep your hands on the wall." He grinds out into my ear. I push my hands harder into the tiles, as he uses a knee to spread my legs apart.

Oh hells yes, I like where this is going.

I can hear my panting breaths get ragged as he circles my swollen clit with his thumb and he strokes my entrance with his fingers.

"Jesus, Cora," he grits, "You are so wet for me."

"I need you, Seb," I breathe. "Please."

He groans into my neck and I can feel his length thrumming against the crease of my ass. He takes his cock in one hand and lines the smooth head up with my pussy.

I clench my teeth together as he rubs himself back and forth through my folds, coating his cock with my slickness. Then he lines himself up again and slides all the way inside me with one sure stroke.

I cry out, trembling as the waves of pleasure tear through me.

He holds me up against him, my sex-addled body practically a dead weight as I hold myself together as much as I can. His chest rumbling against my back, he keeps one of his glorious hands working my clit and the other splayed across my ribs, holding me firmly against his chest. He moves inside me like a tidal wave, our bodies crashing together. My orgasm crests over me fast and implacable, sweeping away anything that came before, shattering my mind, leaving me twitching and breathless as he chases his own release.

"Mine." Seb growls in my ear. I don't even think he

knows he is saying it, branding me as his. My heart is a fluttering creature inside me, elation and warmth swirling alike in my chest, a hot ribbon of connection tying me to this man working my body behind me. The way that I feel right now, sated, treasured, a *belonging* that I have never experienced before, fills me up with the bright and foolish possibility. I *want* to be his for as long as he will have me. He saw my magic and didn't run. He's still here.

"I'm yours, Seb." I whisper. He shudders then, his hips stilling as he comes hard, crushing me into him and gasping.

Chapter 26

Seb

I wake up to warm sunlight on my face, soft hair across my neck and Cora draped naked over my chest.

My Wolf is utterly content, our Mate sleeping safely so close to us. This is a feeling that I wasn't sure I would ever experience. Cora had been so cagey, and I had been such an asshole idiot, both of us made this harder than it had to be. But here we are now, nestled into each other, as we should be.

I hold my body still, inhaling her sweetness, memorizing everything about this moment. Cora grumbles softly in her sleep and shifts her body. She flings an arm up and over her head and settles deeper into my shoulder. Her hair is floating slightly, like there is a soft current making it swim and I marvel that I have never seen it loose before. She always keeps it tied up, hiding her incredible magic. Magic that she used on my body last night. After we had cleaned up a second time in the shower, we stumbled to her bed. She had trailed her fingers over my skin, her

Magic warming her fingertips to nearly scorching as she teased me. My Wolf had loved every fucking minute of it. We had finally succumbed to our exhaustion as the sun was starting to peek over the horizon and we burrowed together under her sheets.

I have never known peace like this before. Always my Wolf has been restless, seeking. As far back as I can remember, I've searched for any information about my parents. It was painful and slow, each time I thought I had discovered a lead, it would vanish like smoke.

Something is keeping them from me, and I can't rest until I know. No one remembers why they left, just that they did. And that's not enough for me. The hazy memories of my childhood serve only to frustrate me. Since stepping into my role as Alpha, the pull to find answers has been stronger, but the results always the same. Nothing to find. It's like they simply weren't there anymore. The ache in my soul won't let me leave it alone though, so for years I have searched, always reaching for something just out of reach.

Coming to Eliza Falls was an admission of defeat. Gamma had sent us here to cool our heels and keep an eye on her best friend. I came here with my tail tucked between my legs because after years of endless searching, I had still found no trace of mom or dad. Even thinking about them felt like holding water, slippery and impossible.

Then we got here, to this absurd, magical little town, and thoughts of my past fell away once we discovered Cora that day at the market, my Wolf's seeking had turned to yearning. Desperate and hungry, knowing that our Mate was close, but that we couldn't touch her, claim her, had felt like torture.

Now, my Wolf sleeps peacefully inside me, and it's all because of her. She opened up to me last night and I wasn't unaware of how hard that must have been for her. I know how it feels to keep a part of yourself hidden. But she did. She showed me her magic and herself and it's a gift that I will treasure for the rest of my days.

Cora's head tilts back a little over my shoulder then, her mouth opening in a soft snore that is quite possibly the cutest thing I have ever seen. Her breath catches in her throat and she snort-coughs herself awake. Blinking her eyes against the light and frowning, she turns her body in towards me and covers her face with the blankets.

"What time is it?" She asks hoarsely, her voice rough from sleep.

I glance at the little analogue clock she has on her dresser across the room.

"12:30 in the afternoon."

"UUUGH that's not enough, wake me up tomorrow." She groans.

I chuckle at her tone. My Mate clearly isn't a morning person.

I hold her against me, cocooned in the nest we made out of her bed last night. Idly stroking my hand up and down along her spine, I continue to marvel over her. Over what we did together. My hand strokes over her skin and Cora shivers.

"Mmmmm that feels really nice." She mumbles into my chest, rubbing her sleepy face into my pectoral.

Blinking up at me, she squints and grumbles again. "Ugh. This really feels too early. Are we getting up?"

I trail my hand down over her bare hip under the blankets and she stills, her gaze locking onto mine.

"Why Seb, what big hands you have." She purrs. She leans forward to kiss me softly on the mouth. When I lick along the seam of hers she shrieks.

"Gah! NO! I have Breath Of The Morning and there

will be no tongues involved until we have both brushed our teeth!"

I laugh as she scrambles out of the blankets, stealing a sheet and tearing the whole mess of fabric onto the floor. She stumbles, catches herself and straightens her shoulders with a snap.

"You sir, will cover *that* up so I can be remotely productive today."

I am still laughing as I look down and see that my morning wood is on full display.

I find myself puttering around in the workshop later that afternoon, unable and unwilling to focus on anything but the last twenty four hours spent with Cora. Everything about her makes my skin feel tight, like I am so full of what I feel about her, there isn't room for anything else.

I left her at her apartment this morning, a tidy two bedroom suite above their shop. Desi came back just after two, as Cora and I were finishing up a late breakfast of toaster strudels and a spicy tea blend that I'm sure Cora makes herself. Desi smiled and kissed Cora's cheek as she swept into the little kitchenette, and I blushed when she swooped down to kiss my cheek as she danced out. She is like a forest spirit, flighty at first glance, but the knowing look she gave me was anything but focused. She had sussed out that we were werewolves, something that we were very conscious of hiding, and that alone had my Wolf's hackles rising once I started thinking about it. She is more powerful than she looks.

Tate saunters into the office a little while later, smirking at me and visibly holding himself back from giving me shit about everything.

"Just say it."

"Dude. Desi is a firecracker. Did you know that she is a

Spirit witch?? That woman can see the fucking future. It's so hot."

I gape at my brother. That is not at all what I was expecting him to say. I cross my arms over my chest and lean against the desk behind me.

"No shit? That explains some things."

Tate leans against the door jam, thumbs tucked into the pockets of his old jeans.

"I like them, the more time I spend with them, the more they feel like Pack, you know?"

I'm surprised again, I had no idea that he and Desi have gotten so close. But as I let my mind wander over the last few months, I realize that my obsession with being near Cora has put us into the path of Desi just as often, and I'm a selfishly obtuse asshole for not thinking about how Tate is handling all of this.

"Hey man, I'm sorry I've been such a dick lately." I say. "I haven't been thinking beyond my own fascination with Cora, and I've been shitty to you."

"What? No way man, she's your true Mate, that shit trumps everything else. I am super happy for you. Especially now that she's official. She is right? You guys finally let loose and got primal right?" He waggles his eyebrows, grinning at me, and I can only roll my eyes at him.

He knows what we've done. He can smell her all over me, and his Wolf will be able to feel how content mine is. He probably heard us back in McLaren the other night. That thought makes me cringe. But I appreciate that he's letting me off the hook. I really have let my preoccupation with her cloud everything else, and I need to at least try to get my head back to normal. But, what even *is* normal? Maybe this is already it. Maybe I'm supposed to be completely gone for her and that's my life now. It certainly feels good to let myself crush on her. Once again, I wish our parents were here to talk about this stuff. This is another problem that I could solve with a chat with a dad over coffee.

But I realize as I look over at my brother, who is now shuffling around the office, dancing to a tune only he can hear, that I have family right in front of me. I just need to open up.

"Want to grab some dinner to take back to Jett?" I ask him.

He keeps dancing, throwing his elbows up and shaking his hips as he turns around to look at me.

"You aren't spending the day with your girl?"

"I can do stuff without her."

"Can you though?" His tone is teasing, but I give myself a minute to think about it. I can. I'm sure of it. My Wolf whines inside me, establishing how he feels about being away from our Mate now that we've completed the bond. I let my attention swing back to Cora and I realize that she has a thread connecting to my Wolf now too. It's warm and sinuous, a glowing strand of swirling purple that flows out from my body. I can see it if I squint just right.

She's Pack after all.

Tate and I collect some savoury buns from Sela at the bakery (I refuse to call it by its name) and walk ourselves across town to Aunt Jett's. She's humming to herself on the front porch as we walk up, and smiles, her cheeks creasing in familiar wrinkles. She really is a wonderful aunt to have, in as much as she's not really our aunt. But I love her like one, so that's all I need to know. She spies the bag in my hands and her smile turns down abruptly.

"Did you boys get into trouble? What did you do?"

Tate and I exchange confused glances.

"You know we wouldn't do anything you wouldn't Jett." Tate winks at her as he leans down to kiss her cheek.

She flicks his ear and he throws an indignant look at me as he scuttles away from her.

"Why bring me offerings then?"

I look down at the bag of buns in my hand and frown. Have I really been so self absorbed all this time that bringing snacks looks suspicious?

"We just wanted to bring you something to add to dinner, Jeez." Tate says, keeping his distance.

"I'm sorry I've been distant lately Aunt Jett, this is probably my fault." I say, handing over the buns.

"Are these from Sela?" She asks, holding the bag up to her face and inhaling deeply.

I nod, and she closes her eyes. "You're forgiven. Did the pink one finally accept you sweetheart?"

I cough, surprised at the quick shift in conversation, and sputter my reply.

"Uh, Cora?"

"Oh course Cora honey, you've been mooning over her since you arrived. She's a lovely witch dear, I approve. I've always wondered if the carpets match the drapes, if you know what I mean. She refuses to join the Midnight Ladies Association so I never get to see her naked."

I honestly have no idea how to respond to this, and look helplessly over at Tate, who is snorting into his sleeve as he tries to smother his laughter.

"I am not at liberty to say Jett."

"Good boy."

Chapter 27

Cora

"Did you know they were werewolves this whole time?"

Desi and I are in the shop on a crisp and glorious Sunday afternoon, finishing up a few inventory requests. Other boutiques carry my line in other towns, and it's one of the aspects of our business that I excel at. I love that I can bring in a little extra income for us outside of the shop since Desi's strengths are so focused inside of it. The shop is closed to customers today so we've been hustling through work orders and clearing the corner of the shop for the beautiful new display Seb is building for us. Every time I think about it, my chest fills with warmth and my thoughts drift to him again.

My thoughts never seem to be too far from him at the best of times now, and I'm not mad about it. It's been a week of a whole new life. Dating a werewolf has turned out to be my new favourite thing. Everything around me feels brighter and more lively. The last few golden leaves on the trees all over town look even more beautiful and the air smells better somehow. I dig it. It feels like there's a magnet inside of me constantly pulling me towards him. I've never felt this way about a relationship before. It's heady and intense, and as much as it is terrifying, I kind of love it. I might love *him*.

A pulse in my chest flares at the thought and my fingertips get tingly. I take some deep breaths to settle my magic, which has been a bit of a spicy bitch lately. It's almost like since opening up to Seb and acknowledging these big feelings inside, feelings that I have always squashed down into a tight little knot of repression before, my magic has felt a teensy bit more intense. I twist the silver band ring on my finger while I focus on my breath, letting my fingers cool off. I've taken to wearing my hair braided tight in a crown this past week, since all the extra juju flaring up in me has made it a little more extroverted than usual.

"Obviously yes, Darling. I'm surprised that it took you so long to figure it out. He positively growls at you on a regular basis." She coos back to me, not in any way ruffled by my tone.

"Also, I knew this would happen eventually, I just hadn't seen when." Her nonchalance is irritating but I find myself deflating. How can I honestly be mad at her when getting down with Seb has made me feel so… good. Like my skin has been itchy and I finally get to scratch it. Like diving into cool water on a steamy summer afternoon. Like connecting that one frustrating puzzle piece, after thinking that perhaps you never would and then the only option is to toss the whole fucker into the wall.

I throw myself dramatically into a chair and huff a sigh. I can't be mad about anything when I replay the dirty shenanigans Seb and I have engaged in over the last few days. Oh Gods he is a *deliciously* dirty perv. I shiver and blush and look back at my best friend.

"I didn't really think about it. He's always so, so… *broody* and weird and it ruffled my feathers so I repressed all thoughts of him." Well, most thoughts of him. Some thoughts.

Oh who am I kidding, I obsessed about him constantly.

"And how did that work out for you, Sweet Tart?" Desi's expression is one of serene satisfaction. Also known as smug as shit.

"Ugh! Don't start. I realize that I've spent nearly a year pining over him and generally wasting all of this time that I could have better spent climbing him like a tree." I roll my eyes but inwardly cringe. I have wasted a lot of time and energy being defensive. And cagey. Perhaps my fierce self-preservation could have been tempered with more emotional reflection? Or any at all? My history with men is shadowed by my fears of rejection. I am aware of this. I did some work with a therapist a few years ago. Deanna is a lovely empath that has a practice in town, and she helped me see that I have some unresolved Daddy issues. But never before has a relationship felt so important. So utterly life-altering. This connection to Seb feels like it could really be something amazing, and all of my baggage is starting to feel heavy again. I don't want him to realize that I am not worth it, that my magic isn't normal. I don't want him to leave too. So I squish my feelings down a little farther each time my magic flares up. Play it cool. If I let myself realize how important he's becoming to me, the risk of pain increases. If I keep it casual, it won't hurt so bad when he comes to his senses.

"Well not to worry, my precious Cupcake, you have the rest of your life to scale the hunky mountain known as Seb."

Wait, what?

"What does that mean? We only just started sleeping together." I ask her, trying to keep my tone cool, but my skin suddenly feels a bit prickly. Desi stops what she is doing and slowly turns to face me, her eyes wide and unblinking.

"His Wolf has claimed you, Cora, that's a pretty major commitment. Like, forever. He told you, didn't he?" She looks puzzled, like I should know this already.

"He may have mentioned something along those lines in the heat of the moment, but I thought it was just that! The heat of the moment!" I'm starting to feel uncomfortable, my chest tight, and dark spots start to float in my vision. My hair is pulling against the tight braid, strands of it escaping it's constraints and swirling around my face. The mugs on the closest display begin to tremble, which only makes me feel worse. It's happening again, I can't control this.

Desi catches the movement out of the corner of her eye and sweeps over to me, her expression firm.

"I've got you, take deep breaths." She is soothing me like I am a cornered animal and frankly that's a little how I feel. How had I brushed what he said aside so easily? Had I wanted to have sex with him so bad that I waved aside the warning he gave me? The warning I acknowledged to his face??

"Oh holy shit, what have I done?" I rasp. My hair is whipping faster now, almost entirely free of my careful control, and Desi is squinting against it as the ends slash at her face.

Seb is stuck with me forever now? Is he going to regret it now that we have surfaced from our days-long sex fest and are faced with stark reality in the cold light of day? Can I be a good Mate? What does that *even mean*?? I am an earth witch who only mostly has a handle on her powers and can a werewolf even Mate a witch? Is he going to wish that I was a wolf too??

"We will deal with that once you calm down, Honeycomb, you are losing control of your magic and we just need to calm you down." Desi is emanating calm, her voice soothing.

I have to calm down. I can feel my magic swirling around me with my heightened emotions and my fingers are starting to feel hot, my throat dry from smoky heat.

I close my eyes and visualize my magic. The bright ball that I use as my focus is pulsing and dark, and I'm startled when I realize that the magic isn't only mine anymore.

What fresh hell is this??

There is a new layer to my visualized bubble that is entirely other, someone else's magic is swirling all over my own, and in my panic, I push against it. It pulses back, sending a ripple of electricity down my arms. What the actual fuck is going on?

I narrow my focus on the interloper and try to lift it from mine, but it's thick and sticky like honey, resistant to being pulled away. I can feel it latching back on, like it's reluctant to be parted from me.

In confused terror I pull hard on my own magic, pulling it into myself and try to yank it away from the foreign energy. But as soon as my magic's light reaches my body, blinding pain shoots into my chest like I'm being electrocuted. I cry out and stagger backwards.

Chapter 28

Seb

I am a man transformed. Never in my life have I felt so easy in my own skin.

My Wolf is lounging like a happy drunk inside me and nothing can get me down. The air smells sweeter, the breeze feels fresher, everything I look at is inspiring, and even the imperious chickens can't shift my good mood.

Tate and I are at the workshop this afternoon, working on the finishing touches of the display for Cora and Desi.

Cora.

Her soft hair, her endless eyes and her delicate skin. Skin that I have explored every inch of in the last few days with my hands, my mouth.

We've spent a good part of every day together since that night in McLaren's Wood. We've fallen deep into each other. It's only because we both have jobs that will no longer wait for us that we have come up for air at all. Even now, I'm only barely paying attention to the oil I'm rubbing into the finished piece. In my mind, I'm smoothing oil into Cora's soft skin, moans escaping from her kiss-bruised mouth.

"Dude." Tate says sharply.

I stiffen and turn to look at my brother. He's looking at me with exasperation, and I guess that he's been talking for a little while already.

"Sorry, what?" I'm only partly embarrassed that I'm not really paying attention.

"I appreciate that you are new to this whole Blissfully Coupled Existence thing, but you're getting ridiculous."

I cock an eyebrow at him. "How am I ridiculous? I've just been working on this piece all morning."

"Yeah, and you've oiled that leg three times."

I look down, and sure enough, Tate is right. I'll have to oil the whole piece over again to even out the finish.

Chuckling to myself, (what else can I do) I move away from the piece and wipe my hands off on a clean rag. Grabbing my glass of water I take a long pull.

Tate's phone pings an incoming message and I turn back to the display. We've really outdone ourselves on this piece, and I'm not ashamed to admit that the idea of pleasing Cora has given me extra inspiration. My Wolf is desperate to take care of her, and this display is a small step to fulfilling that need.

Inhaling a deep breath to shake off my lingering daydream, I pick up the oilcloth again. As I bend over the bare legs to start finishing them, I feel a tug in my chest and my Wolf snarls in dismay. Frowning, I look up sharply and see Tate, staring at me over his phone.

"What is it?" I demand.

"We need to get to the girl's shop, right now." He bites out, turning quickly to grab the van keys.

"I'll drive," he says, voice tight.

Another sharp tug at my Wolf magic and I realize

belatedly that it's the Bond with Cora pinging like an alarm. A desperate chill flashes over my bones.

What is she doing?

I jump to my feet and race after Tate to the truck. My Wolf is snarling inside me now, frantic to get to our Mate. I can feel her pulling on the Mate Bond, pulling away from us and I can't understand why. I need to shift, suddenly and desperately I know I need to be in my Wolf shape to protect Cora.

"Pull up into the side alley when we get there." I grit out, my change prickling under my skin. Tate nods and I throw myself into the back of the cube van, my body already changing.

Heaving great lungfuls of air while the van swerves through traffic, I briefly send out a prayer that we don't get pulled over. Explaining a giant Wolf in the back of a speeding van isn't something that we need to deal with right now.

I release my tight control over my change and the Wolf bursts out of me. I lay panting on the floor of the truck for just a moment, before scrabbling up to stand behind Tate. He pulls quickly into the side alley and I leap out of the van, racing towards the shop's back door. It isn't locked and I throw my big body against it to get through.

The heavy door swings open and smashes against the inside wall with a crash and a shower of drywall. I can hear Desi's harsh breathing as I round the corner and practically skid to a halt when I see the scene in front of me.

Cora is levitating in the right-hand corner of the room, shards of broken pottery swirling around her, her hair whipping all over her face. Her eyes are screwed tight and it looks like she is in pain. Desi is on the ground behind the counter, bright blood running down one side of her face, and I watch Tate run over to her and wrap her in his arms to shield her.

I snarl at the chaos in front of me, and Desi sniffs and calls out.

"She doesn't realize it's you! She had a little moment of panic earlier when she realized that the Mate Bond is forever, and her magic flared."

My Wolf howls in agony as I take in what Desi said.

Cora doesn't want me.

I don't understand. It feels like my soul is shattering in pieces all around me. The fire in my chest intensifies and I feel Cora pull on the bond again, trying to separate herself from my Wolf, from me. I howl in anguish. A light touch on my flank has me swirling around, teeth bared.

"It's ok Seb," Desi hushes me. She reaches up and puts her small hands on my muzzle.

"She's panicking because she doesn't understand that the bond is permanent, not because she doesn't want it. Our girl has some baggage that fucks with her head, but she's gone for you. When her magic flared and she looked inside to settle it, the new magic she found frightened her. She doesn't realize that the new magic is the Bond with you. She's been fighting against it because she thinks it's an enemy but I can't reach her. You need to get to her, Seb, before she burns herself out. She needs to understand to accept it. She needs you."

I shudder at Desi's words, understanding flowing over me. Cora has been protecting herself, keeping herself separate and safe the whole time I've known her. Of course she would pull away from a strange magic she found inside her. In all the time we have spent together over the last few days, consummating our new relationship, I didn't consider that she wouldn't know about how tangible the bond between us would be. What it would feel like inside her.

I've just been luxuriating in it, assuming that she feels the same.

Remorse for my own shortsightedness fills me and I turn back to Cora. She looks terrified, her magic swirling around her as she thrashes in the air, the temperature around us steadily increasing. This whole corner of the shop looks like a tornado has blown through, but I'll let myself be awestruck at just how much power she's wielding another time. Right now I have to find a way to reach her before she literally starts a fire.

Chapter 29

Cora

I have never been more scared in my entire life.

I didn't even know that separate magic could combine with my own. How could this have happened without me knowing it? Everything has been feeling so, so good. Seb and I have finally gotten over ourselves, and Gods dammit I love him, and I will never get to tell him now!

This other magic won't get away from me. I'm getting exhausted as I continue to try to pull it away from myself. But it hurts, holy shit, it hurts *so much!* Every time I pull the pulsing, sticky magic off of mine, it fucking hurts like I am ripping my own nails out. My fingers are throbbing, the fire inside me pushing to get out even as I force it to stay in. Never before has it felt so hard to control. I feel desperate and horrified that I am losing the fight to contain it. It's crackling at the edges of my skin, and I can't let it out. Everything I have worked so hard for will be destroyed if I release it and I am shaking with the effort to keep it all inside.

I can't keep fighting this strange magic forever though. I can hear sobbing now, gut-wrenching, painful sobs and I blink my eyes open and look around. I realize that the sobbing is me. I am weeping out loud while I pull at my magic over and over again. I wish I could tell Seb that I'm sorry. That I've been so happy in the short time we've been together and that I've never felt this way about anyone before. Like I've finally come home when he is inside me, when he holds me in his arms.

As if wishing makes it come true, I gasp as I see Seb in his Wolf form in front of me. He's slowly padding towards me, like I'm a predator about to strike.

I inhale sharply at the irony of his big Wolf being wary of me. It sends a surge of despair into my gut; I'm too dangerous to keep him. He's going to leave too. He should!

He freezes and watches me for a moment. We stare into each other's eyes and I will him to protect himself.

"Seb!" I choke out, unable to stop crying.

The air around him shimmers, and then my Seb is standing there, his broad shoulders slightly hunched forward like he is protecting his core.

He's breathing hard, still holding my gaze, and it breaks my heart to know that I had a chance with him for something great. That we could have been amazing together, but our chance for happiness is gone. This strange magic isn't letting go of me, and I can't think straight to fight it anymore.

"Cora," Seb whispers. The tenacious new magic pulses inside of me, and I thrash against it. I just want this last moment with him! He clears his throat and continues louder. "Cora, babe, I need you to let me in."

What the fuck?

"W-what?" I'm utterly confused. What is he talking about? I'm losing my hold on the magic and it's taking everything I have to contain it within me. I know that I have already lashed out, that my storm has already taken its toll on the space around me. The slash across Desi's temple fills me with self-loathing, a shard of broken pottery whipped past her and I will never forgive myself. Hopefully she can forgive me someday for destroying this side of the shop.

I blink my focus back to the man in front of me and see that Seb has inched closer.

"Stop, Seb! Don't come any closer to me; I can't hold this in for much longer! You all need to leave, I'm not safe!" I cry. My face is streaked with tears and I'm trembling from the exertion.

"I'm not going *anywhere.*" He growls. I can feel his fury pushing against my skin through all of the turmoil. I startle at his ferocity. I don't know what to do with this right now.

"The magic you are fighting is MINE!" He practically roars at me.

"What? What are you talking about?! This magic is soaking into me, Seb, I can't get it off my own! I can't control any of it anymore."

"It's the Mate Bond, Cora. You are fighting against *me.* You are trying to pull us apart and it's hurting you. Please, *please,* Cora, let me in."

I'm completely lost. This makes no sense! I've never heard of a Mate Bond being a tangible thing. This new energy pulsing over top of my magic is *solid.* I can feel it sliding over mine, it's moving inside me like a swirl of cold water. That can't be normal. Have I been fighting so hard to separate my magic from Seb's this whole time? I take a shuddering breath in and hold it, trying to calm my racing pulse.

I close my eyes and look inward at my magic agan. I can still see my own ball of blue light, and swirling over top of it is a thick cloud of inky purple and silver. I try to calm my frantic heart and really look at it again. Gently turning it over in my mind.

The smokey, dark swirls are coiling around my little ball of light, but as I look at it more closely now, it isn't invading. I don't feel any malice; it's *caressing*. I reach out to touch the new magic again, and the familiar scent of pine and earth flows around me. It *is* Seb!

Oh my Gods, I nearly destroyed our Bond and my magic and my fucking day job because I *overreacted*?? I groan out loud, humiliation and disgust washing over me in a deluge, and stop fighting. I let it swirl around me and envelope me and I breathe the Mate Bond deep into myself. I can feel his Wolf all over my body now, testing the bond and huffing his deep, warm breath into all my nooks and crannies. How could I have missed that it was Seb's Wolf this *whole time*?

Releasing my desperate hold on everything, my magic finally escapes my body in a burst of heat and a thrashing squall that tears at everything around me. I hear the windows groaning under the pressure until it settles abruptly. I shudder and drop to the floor, landing awkwardly on my back.

"Cora!" Seb yells, as he rushes to catch me.

His big body drops next to mine and he pulls me into his lap.

"Cora please, I'm so sorry, I should have told you more about the Bond, what it means." He moans hoarsely into my neck. His strong arms surround me like a fortress and I let him rock me back and forth, too exhausted to pull away.

"No, Seb, I'm sorry too. I freaked out when Desi

confirmed that the Bond was forever and I thought that you'd regret it and I panicked. Then I tried to not panic and when I saw the unfamiliar magic over top of mine, I really freaked out. I'm so sorry." I babble, barely coherent through my tears.

"Never, Cora." Seb's hot eyes sear into mine then, "I will never regret our Bond. I am yours and I will *never* let you go."

Fresh tears spill over my cheeks and I give in to them, letting the sobs wrack my worn-out body. I'm exhausted, emotionally and physically, my heart is overfull and I'm... going to pass out? Is this what fainting feels like? My limbs go numb, a ringing starts up in my ears and the darkness on the edges of my vision creeps in, quickly taking over everything until there is nothing but black.

Chapter 30

Seb

My Wolf is prowling around the edges of my mind, grumbling low in my chest as we hold Cora while she sleeps.

It's been three days since she flipped her fucking lid. Three days since she nearly destroyed the business she and Desi have worked so hard to build. Three long days of hovering over her while she recovers from the fight of our lives. She woke up for a little while, mumbled an awkward apology, burst into tears and then let me hold her until she cried herself asleep again.

Desi and Tate have been downstairs repairing the damage in the shop, never too far away. Upon inspection, it had turned out to only need surface repairs. They are down some damaged inventory, but other than that, it isn't anything a little drywall plaster and fresh paint won't fix.

I haven't left Cora's side since we settled here in her room, other than to eat quickly and run to the bathroom. My Wolf won't allow it. Even when Alma stormed in yesterday, concern and resolve etched on her pale face, I didn't leave Cora's side. Alma had narrowed her eyes on me, taking in my own ragged state, and we quietly staged our battle of wills, neither of us willing to back down, both of us fighting for the same thing. Finally she nodded, approval in her expression, and then sat down next to Cora's still form. I watched as she pulled a simple gold ring from her pocket, and gently exchanged it for the silver ring that Cora always wore. She held her hands over it, Cora's hand in hers, and I felt a wave of energy flow out of Alma.

"She mustn't take this off; it helps contain her storm. I gave her the silver one when she was struggling as a teenager, but the magic of the Mate Bond is increasing her gifts. I didn't want her to fear herself, so I didn't tell her before, and I'm unsure if I want to tell her now. It might be best if she knows this time, but I can't see the right path forward."

She reached out to softly brush Cora's tangled hair off her face, and I watched her. Her love was so clear and palpable, it sent a pang of longing through me. I wish I could remember more of my own mother; I believe in my soul that she would love Cora too.

"She's going to retreat into herself when she wakes up. It's how she deals with big feelings." Alma said softly. I raised an eyebrow, waiting for her to continue. She sighed, and I watched her decide to trust me.

"She blames herself for her father leaving us." She looked sharply at me then. "It's rubbish, the man left because we weren't the family that his mother wanted. Not because of her, he loved her." She smoothed Cora's hair again, tender touches that showed more softness from this formidable woman than I'd ever seen before.

"His family had very specific expectations for him, and getting a witch pregnant by accident at nineteen wasn't one of them. I told him I didn't need him to martyr himself for us, but he did what he thought was right at the time. Until his family's connections and reach got too close to us. His mother was a powerful woman with public aspirations, and she had a wife lined up for him. Cora and I were never a part of her plan."

I just listened, understanding that she wasn't necessarily saying all of this for my benefit alone.

"As humans love to do, they threatened him, through our girl. Sent horrifying messages, the last arriving the day he left, they went to his office with photos of her at school. So he left in the night. His timing was fucking terrible. I didn't want her to be afraid, so I didn't tell her the truth. But I was wrong. She's blamed herself ever since and hidden her magic as much as she can. I didn't realize how much until years later, watching her shut down instead of falling in love. I'm telling you this so you understand where she is coming from. Don't let her push you away." I snorted at that. Like anything could keep us away from her now.

"Do you know what I am?" I asked her. She arched her own eyebrow then, as she nodded.

"Then you know that I will never leave my Mate. For anything. I am hers, forever."

Her eyes filled with tears, and she reached across Cora's still sleeping form to squeeze my hand.

She composed herself and then quietly left, with instructions to not fuck it up.

But I won't. We nearly lost her, our True Mate, and the bond that tethers our souls together, because I didn't just talk to her about it, and that is a mistake I will never make again. Neither Cora or I are great at communication. A wasted year of yearning and retreating whenever either of us got close is a testament to that fact. But I will see to it that we are always open with each other going forward. Nothing matters but her.

So I wait. I hold her and listen when she cries, and I'll tell her whatever she wants to know, every day, for the rest of my life.

As we lay here in her bed hours later, tangled together in the sheets with the sunlight just creeping over the horizon through her window, Cora starts to stir. Her breathing changes as she takes in a deep breath and she slowly blinks her eyes open. I meet her sleepy gaze with my own, locking us together in this small way.

"Mmm, morning." She mumbles, her voice husky from days of tears and sleep. She smiles, just a gentle curve of her lips, as my Wolf purrs at her in my chest. Just seeing that small smile washes away the fear and anxiety of the last few days. She is safe in our arms and everything will be ok.

"How are you feeling?" I ask her softly. I don't want to break the spell that she has woven over us, just by holding my gaze.

"Better. Embarrassed honestly. I keep thinking to myself how I jumped to a very intense and potentially unhinged conclusion and nearly tore the store apart with a magical panic attack."

She cringes as she says it, clearly still feeling the sting of her reaction.

"You were scared, and you didn't have all of the information."

I don't hold her behaviour against her. I acknowledge that yes, it was pretty intense. But in my time getting to know her, Cora has proven herself to be a firecracker; her fierce spirit and quietly wild nature don't frighten me. Werewolves can't throw stones about wild behaviour.

"I should have told you what the Mate Bond would feel

like. I should have known that you might not know. It was irresponsible of me. I am so sorry, Cora." I say quietly.

"It's ok. I'm sorry that I didn't tell you about how extra my magic is. I usually keep it under better control." Her voice is barely a whisper. Snuggling her body further into mine, she avoids making eye contact. I wrap my arms tighter around her, holding her against me.

After a moment, she heaves a deep breath and lifts her head back so she can look at me again.

"I know that you told me there would be no going back, that night in the woods. I think on some level I understood it. But there was a small part of me that doubted that you would want to be tied to me forever like that." She confesses, her voice small, timid. Nothing like her fierce spirit. I hate it.

My Wolf growls at the notion. She is ours and we are hers and I frown darkly at her.

Her chuckle is soft and scratchy. "I get it now though. When I was fighting against the bond, it was like I was fighting myself, I couldn't get anywhere and it hurt like a motherfucker." She takes a couple of deep breaths and starts again.

"And then you were there. And when I stopped fighting it, when I let you in… everything clicked into place. The pain went away. My magic settled and I am so, so grateful that you are still here giving me a chance to show you that I am in. All in."

With shining eyes, she shifts our bodies so that she is lying across me. She leans down and kisses me on the mouth. I can feel her trembling, all of her fear and longing and hope in that kiss.

I slowly trail my hands up her shoulders and hold her face in my palms.

"I will keep all of you Cora. I will spend the rest of our lives showing you every day that I am yours."

I press my lips to hers, the salty taste of her tears reminding me that this woman bared her heart to me, even though she was afraid. I am honoured and respectful of that trust. I vow to show her every day just how much. I kiss her, slow and deep, my heart and my Wolf and my promise in my kiss.

The end.

Thank you so much for reading my book! I hope you loved it because I had a blast writing it.

Want to find out what happens next for Cora and Seb? Sign up here for their exclusive bonus epilogue!
(https://www.subscribepage.com/omm-bonus-epilogue-sign-up)

Did you love this book? Please consider leaving a review! Reviews really helps other readers find the books you love and encourages us authors to keep writing these fun stories.

Want more Eliza Falls and to follow along with me on this writing adventure? Check out my website at…
https://www.maggiefrancis.com
I've got lots of plans up my sleeve and I'm really excited to share them with you!
xox

follow me on Instagram, I post there regularly. :)
@maggie.francis.books

I'm so grateful and beyond excited to have you here on this adventure. I hope you enjoyed Cora & Seb and their cagey love story. I loved writing them and letting them live in my head for a while.
I want to give a shout out to a few people who helped this project get off the ground and made it what it is…
Big thanks to Brenna Davies and Amy Ollerton, two lovely and talented editors who whipped my ridiculous novella into shape and were so kind to me THE WHOLE TIME.
My Mom, for all the support throughout this whole process and for handing me my first romance novel back in the day… who'd have thought I'd write my own??

Sandra, you gods damned delight. Yeah, I'm looking at you.
My Bookclub Babes, I have many tender feelings for you. Like, a lot.
Kaisha, our BizBabes meetings make me feel like a human, xox.
Jina, your vision helped the cover be just what it needs to be!
To everyone who beta read for me and cheered me on and fed the beast that is Maggie, things are just going to get better and more fun!
Seriously, I don't think I can put all this back in.
To the author friends I've made along the way, thank you for answering my questions and generally being awesome. I feel lucky to be getting to know you!

And to my husband and kids, who I love more than I can say, this is for you.
Only, the kids can't read this until, like…never. Probably never.

xox
Maggie

Manufactured by Amazon.ca
Bolton, ON